SWEET GIRL

CRISTIN HARBER

ISBN-10: 1-942236-42-5
ISBN-13: 978-1-942236-42-9

www.CristinHarber.com

Published in the United States of America

BOOKS BY CRISTIN HARBER

THE TITAN SERIES:

Book 1: Winters Heat (Colby Winters)

Book 1.5: Sweet Girl (Prequel to Garrison's Creed)

Book 2: Garrison's Creed (Cash Garrison)

Book 3: Westin's Chase (Jared Westin)

Book 4: Gambled (Brock Gamble)

Book 5: Chased (Asher McIntyre)

Book 6: Savage Secrets (Rocco Savage)

Book 7: Hart Attack (Roman Hart)

Book 8: Black Dawn (Parker Black)

THE DELTA SERIES:

Book 1: Delta: Retribution

Book 2: Delta: Revenge

THE ONLY SERIES:

Book 1: Only for Him

Book 2: Only for Her

Book 3: Only for Us

Book 4: Only Forever

ACKNOWLEDGMENTS

Thank you to my beautiful, supportive family. I have nothing without your love.

Thank you for all the Titan readers who first fell in love with Cash and Nicola in Garrison's Creed. I fell right along with you, and when the idea of this story first came into play, I could not wait to get started. I wouldn't be able to do what I love without the Titan readers, especially those who hang out on the Team Titan page. Every day I smile and laugh (and drool) because of you.

I have tons of hugs and thanks for my critique partners. Every time I have an idea, you push me.

Rox: Thank you for your speed and commitment. I value all your suggestions and love to pump up the emotion just to see if you'll give me a thumbs up.

Shex: Every devil horn chapter, I push myself knowing you will have your critter way with me. I appreciate all of the insight and suggestions.

Dia: You make me smile and laugh when I'm ready to choke on a deadline. I'm lucky to have your candid advice and expert story telling skills. Love ya.

Sparks: WWMBD. You inspire and push me to be better. You're my friend, my cohort, and the recipient of my AAPs. I'm lucky to have you. Thank you for everything.

Karen Allen at Red Adept, thank you for the wonderful guidance and consistent help. I love your eagle eyes and virtual red pen.

Cover designer extraordinaire Kim Killion of Hot Damn Designs, thank you and your team for what your do best: gorgeous covers that make thumbnails jump off the screen!

CHAPTER 1

NICOLA STOOD INSIDE THE DORM lobby of Miller Hall and leaned against a bulletin board. With her heart beating faster than it should, she plotted her escape outside and through the pack of squealing girls. If there was one thing she knew about Chesterfield College, it was that high-pitched squeaks could only mean one thing: her brother Roman and his best friend Cash had arrived.

They were her favorite friends. But right about now, she was pretty sure they were standing on the brick ledge near the front door, using their legendary campus status to their advantage and creating an eye-roll worthy scene. They loved the ridiculous attention. She'd give them hell about that later.

Today was the day the dorms opened for fall semester. During her freshmen year, Nicola had thought the Romans and Cashes of campus stood outside Miller Hall to be helpful, welcoming, blah, blah, but now she knew better. They were trolling to meet their soon-to-be latest conquests.

She threw her bag over her shoulder, glancing at her baggy t-shirt and flip-flops, definitely not what the gaggle would be wearing. Not that she cared. Much.

1

Nicola tamped down the smidge of self-doubt, shook her head, and charged. She rounded the corner and saw she'd been right. Cash and Roman perched on the ledge. Girls jockeyed for front-row positions like groupies. Roman and Cash played to their audience of short-shorts and push-up bras with jokes and flirty smiles. An abandoned sign lay by their feet. *TKX Rush Party. Ladies Drink Free*. Clearly, the boys didn't need signage for attention.

Nic would be at the party tonight, just as she had been at all the others. She usually had fun, and she, Roman, and Cash were inseparable most times. Now that she was back on campus, it made sense to show. But seriously, the whole screaming chick thing? Lusting after Roman and Cash like they were campus rock stars? She didn't want to watch any of it. Ever.

Cash's straw cowboy hat dipped low, covering his face. Shaggy blond hair stuck out and made his country cool guy look work in so many ways. She hadn't seen him for the last few weeks. She'd kept missing him back home, and with her trying to nab the internship she wanted, and him being such a damn party boy, it'd been weeks. Somehow, he'd gotten broader and taller, and she made it even more of a point to ignore him.

Sort of.

She peeked. Damn, Cash… Was he even tanner? Was his hair blonder? Her stomach jumped into her throat. If Roman knew what crossed her mind when it came to Cash, he'd lock her up in their parents' basement.

And if Cash ever knew? She knotted her fingers together because that was a no-go. He could never know. It would ruin everything.

"Hey, Nic." From the top of the brick wall, Cash's drawl slid right down her spine. He hadn't yelled over his crowd of groupies, just used his laidback, easy-going drawl that drove her to distraction. "Wait up."

An audible grumble rippled through the crowd until Roman shouted, "Who's coming tonight?"

The crowd cheered. Nicola rolled her eyes and kept moving toward the student activity center, dubbed the SAC, to hit the cafeteria. Focusing on lunch and not on the army of floozies seemed like a better idea.

"Nicola." Cash was behind her, but she kept going. "Nic." He stepped in front of her, grabbed her waist, then threw her over his shoulder. "What, you can't hear me? I haven't seen you in weeks. What's a guy got to do to get your attention?"

She almost laughed at the irony, but she was upside down and remembering how insanely amazing he always smelled. "I'm hungry, Cash. Put me down."

"Me too." He plodded up the long ramp in front of the SAC with her still over his shoulder.

She could've stared at his backside and not complained, except she was scared she'd melt into a puddle of goo. "Put me down."

"Nah." He rolled up the ramp like he didn't have her upside down, and she tried to keep her flip-flops on her feet.

"Come on, Cash." She kicked. He kept his even pace. She went limp. He didn't notice. "I can walk, you know."

"I know. You're coming tonight, right?" He turned his head. His lips tickled her skin like he was having a conversation with her thigh.

"Not totally into seeing you and Roman get pawed all night. So maybe. Maybe not."

Cash stopped and dropped her down in front of him. *Whoa.* Her head spun as the blood rushed back into place. His hands stayed on her waist, steadying her, lingering…

Nope. Cut it out. She shook her head. She'd made it years without getting caught up in the Cash-machine. Slightly caught up, maybe. But not a *look at his hair, stare at his shoulders, and notice that his hands were still on her waist* kinda caught up.

"Jealous." He cocked an eyebrow, and his stunning blue eyes sparkled. "You'll be okay, Sprout."

At that very moment, she decided she hated *Sprout.* Was there a stupider nickname? "Not a chance."

He took a step closer, hands still on her hips. They were locked in a moment, and she didn't know why. Tension burned hot, but it had nothing to do with the summer sun.

"Whoa. Nicola Hart. Missed you, girl." A booming baritone called from behind them. "Summer did your body good."

Her eyes left Cash's only long enough to see Jacob, Chesterfield's quarterback, with two girls, Mira and Jaycee, draped on his arms. Nic could see why they fawned over him. He was cute enough, funny enough, interested in her enough, but she couldn't see him as more than a friend.

She smiled at him and ignored the girls. "Hey, J."

"Ladies." Cash locked an arm around Nic's neck. "Double-deuce."

Jacob pulled an arm from around Jaycee and tugged his number twenty-two jersey twice with a chin lift, like a white

4

boy paying homage to some football god somewhere. "What's up, Cash?"

Nicola was ninety-nine percent sure that both guys, separately, had been with both girls, probably not separately, at one time or another. Good for them. Whatever. She didn't care.

"I'm hungry, boys." She ducked out of Cash's hold. "See ya."

Pushing through the doors, she ditched Cash with Jacob and the set of Tits McGees. Her stomach turned, and Nic lied to herself, saying it was hunger pangs.

Coming from the other direction, she saw Brandy, her best-friend-slash-roommate, who she loved sometimes, hated other times, but who had never left her in a bind. Brandy's bitchiness was a comforting constant.

"Nicola!"

"Hi—"

Brandy bounced on the balls of her feet. "Major. Life. Event. Ready?"

A happy, giddy Brandy was out of the ordinary. "What's going on?"

"We're moving off campus."

"Um, no." Nicola shook her head. "We just moved back *on* campus."

"We've got two weeks until school starts. All this Greek, sports, student activity bullshit has everyone here early with nothing to do, so *I* did us a big favor and found a super cute little house."

Always the responsible one, Nicola could only offer one answer. "No."

"And it has a pool!"

"*No*. Are you kidding me?"

Brandy bounced on her toes again. "So dead serious, I can't even stand it."

"Brandy. Seriously. We can't afford it."

"And it has a kitchen. A bathroom where you don't need shower shoes."

Nicola shook her head. "Not-uh." But a kitchen and a non-shoed shower experience might be what tipped her from *no way* to *all right*.

Brandy paged through a packet in her hand. "It's a sublet. Some associate professor got a better gig somewhere else. It's perfect. Plus, Hannah hasn't moved on campus yet. It's a three bedroom, and she's in if we do it."

Living with another one of her best girl friends would be fun. Brandy held up a picture, and Nic stared. "It seriously has a pool?"

"It has a pool!" Her roomie squealed and showed her a dozen more pictures.

"No." She thought that bathroom shot might do her in. Habit had made Nicola's automatic answer no. But this one… Maybe it was worth thinking about.

Brandy read her mind and started the hard sell. "We don't even have to take care of the pool. That's a bonus. Someone just shows up and cleans it. I already called and asked. It's a five-minute drive from school. We can still get out of our dorms because school hasn't started yet. Full refund. That's a first and last month's rent deposit!"

"We can't." But they actually could if the advertised rent on the listing was correct. Brandy really had thought this out.

"I'm really hating you right now, Nic."

"I hate you most times, so we're even."

"But when you don't, you love me." Her voice was sing-song. "I'm your bitch, bitch. Come on already. Don't make me beg."

Six feet of solid muscle strolled up behind Brandy. "Yeah, Nic. Don't make Brandy beg."

Brandy rolled her eyes and swung her elbow back, catching him in the stomach and making him laugh. "Cash will agree. Tell her to say yes."

"Say yes to Brandy." He passed her roomie and locked his arm back around Nic's neck as the three of them walked into the cafeteria. "To what, anyway?"

"We're moving off campus!" Brandy jumped up on her toes. Again. "And we have a pool!"

"Oh, hell no." Cash stopped so abruptly his arm choked Nicola for a second. "No."

Brandy scowled. "Damn it, Cash."

"No?" God, she hated it when he and Roman got all bossy. "Why not?"

Brandy squealed. "Love it when you two fight."

He ignored her. "No."

Now it was certain yes. "Gimme a copy of the lease, Brandy. I'll sign."

Cash shook his head, and his face turned serious. "No way, no how are you living off campus. You need that little security guard posted on the first floor. And no boys spending the night. And—"

Brandy's head fell back. "You two are a hot mess."

Nic's jaw dropped. "Are you kidding me?"

"Your brother won't let it happen," Cash growled.

So the hell what? "Roman isn't in charge of me."

"Then your dad won't."

"What are you going to do, call him?"

"If that's what it takes." He crossed his arms. "You're a daddy's girl. You might have him wrapped around your finger, but he'd never agree to this. Never."

"You aren't my brother, *and* you can't call my dad when I make decisions you don't like. I'm twenty flipping years old, and if I want to move off campus, you aren't stopping me."

Brandy clapped her hands. "So final decision, we're moving off campus? Please say yes, Nic."

"Yes. Absolutely."

Cash's jaw flexed. "No."

"Do I have to say it again? You're not in charge of me. You're not my brother—"

"Go away, Brandy." Cash stepped closer. "Nic and I need a minute."

Brandy scoffed. "We'll do the deposit later today."

"Sounds good." Nicola tried to sidestep Cash. Didn't work. He bumped her back, stepping closer and closer, until she'd retreated all the way to the glass wall separating the cafeteria from the SAC. It was cold on her shoulders, and Cash was hot to her chest. Her heart raced, and her throat went dry.

"What?" she whispered.

"I'm not your brother."

The pounding in her lungs somehow made it into her ears. It was all she could hear, and it made breathing feel forced and heavy. "I know."

He stared down at her, and the world was lost. This was so bad. He was yelling at her for whatever reason, and the only thing she could see was how full his lips were, how gorgeous his eyes were. Cash put one hand above her shoulder, caging her. Breathing was now a lost art. She didn't remember how.

"I don't like it." His voice rumbled.

"You guys haven't—" She tried to take a breath, and, God, she sounded like one of those screaming girls at Cash's feet, breathy and pathetic. "Lived on campus since you were freshmen."

"Exactly."

She swallowed. "I don't know what that means."

"Fine, Sprout. You don't need—"

"I *hate* Sprout."

He pulled back a couple inches. She couldn't feel the warmth of his breath on her cheek anymore and hadn't noticed it until it was gone.

He gave her a half-grin. "Oh yeah, since when?"

Since he'd had her over his shoulder.

"Christ, Cash." Jacob stepped up behind them. "Give the girl some room. Not everyone's trying to jump in bed with you."

Cash spun so fast she thought it was a joke. "Shut the fuck up."

"Easy, dude." Roman walked over, eyeing their two friends. "Hey, Nic."

Thank God he hadn't seen Cash pushed up against her, not that he'd have a problem with Cash because he never would've guessed what was rolling through her head. But Roman would've called her out for being flustered. He would've laughed. Cash would've laughed. And she would've died.

"Crazy ass." Jacob shook his head, blowing Cash off with a laugh and headed off with Roman toward food.

Cash turned back to her, and his throat bobbed. Shifting in her flip-flops, Nicola felt too damn hot when he looked at her. She always did, and one day, she'd stop fooling herself. It was one-sided, and there was no point in being in love with a guy who was that overprotective and would always think of her as Sprout.

"Nicola." Tray in hand, Jacob walked backward toward the food. "Tonight's TKX party, wanna pre-game at my place? I'll scoop you up around eight?"

Nicola looked at Cash. His strained jaw and thin, flat smile said ten kinds of confusing things. One half of Tits McGee from earlier walked up behind him, wrapping her arm around his waist.

"Sound good, J." Nicola smiled at Cash, at Tits, then walked around him, and wanted to cry.

CHAPTER 2

CASH WATCHED NICOLA WALK OUT of the SAC. Her little butt swayed on a mission to get the hell away from him. Anxiety vibrated inside him, and his palms itched to grab her, or at the very least, push off Mira. Rubbing her boobs on his back with her hand on his stomach, the girl was a collegiate pro at flirting.

Half the cafeteria would drop their girl for a tumble with Mira and her never-that-far-away best friend, Jaycee. They were a lot of fun. He knew first hand. More than once. But really, they were all plastic and party, no substance. Probably, they had some smarts in their pretty little heads, but not when it came to holding a conversation with him. It was all, *hey watch us*.

Jaycee joined them, hooking onto his other side, and the girls chatted about who knew what, probably about the party later that night or some party the night before. That was the extent of their conversations. He figured that they assumed they'd end up with him tonight, but watching a pissed-off Nicola storm down the ramp made his gut churn. This was getting old.

He squinted through the giant windows, watching Nicola move farther away. He wasn't oblivious to her attitude problem or its root cause, and if the girls on his arms weren't Jaycee and Mira, they would've been someone else. It always worked out, and for the most part, no one ever gave him shit for being himself. But it was all a lie.

"Excuse me, ladies." He maneuvered from their hold and jogged after Nic.

It only took a few seconds to catch her. Her power-walking had slowed, and even as he enjoyed the view, he needed to hold her more than he needed to take in the scenery. Lately, the urge to hold her had been getting stronger. It'd always been there but…her long blonde hair was damn near making him stupid.

"Sprout." *Shit.* "Nicola."

Her arms started pumping into a power-walk again. Damn if that didn't make her the cutest thing on campus. He already knew that, though. Everyone did, everyone but Roman, and because of that, Nicola Hart was a no-way, no-how. That, and she'd been his friend his whole life.

He shook his head. *Can't even think like that, man.*

Still she wouldn't get away with running from him just because Mira and Jaycee wanted to put on a show for the lunch crowd.

"Nic." He grabbed her waist, spun her around. "Hey—"

Her eyes were watery and red. In a flash, they morphed to angry. "Leave me alone, Cash."

"Are you—" Was Nicola *crying*? The toughest girl he knew? No way. He'd known her for years and never a tear. Not when the poor kid fell off her bike trying to keep up with

12

him and Roman. Not when they'd convinced her to chew the hottest peppers they could find. And any time he'd ever thought her feelings might be the least bit slighted, Cash had made it his personal mission to handle whatever or whoever made her sweet smile waver.

Nic pushed him away. "Go away."

"Hey, hey, hey." He snagged her arm and let her flail, standing there, ignoring her requests for release. "You done yet?"

Nicola looked away. "Yes. Fine. Done. Can I go now?"

"What's with the waterworks?"

"I'm hormonal. Moving off campus, nostalgia, and all that."

Time ticked, and he didn't believe her. Not that he could do anything about it. Seriously, he needed to get his head on straight. If there was the chance she was teary over him, he needed to walk away and regroup, figure out how to make everything best buds, cool friends between them. It'd kill him if he hurt her. Just kill him.

"Alright." Working his jaw back and forth, he still couldn't let go of her arm.

They stood there, connected, with his hand wrapped around her bicep. Not talking. Not looking. The occasional jock or sorority girl walked by. Said hey. Unconsciously, his thumb smoothed over her skin, making his eyelids sink shut. The quietest gasp fell from her lips. He heard it, savored it, opened his eyes to meet her chocolate brown ones. They were stuck in a moment that wouldn't quit.

Then she tugged her arm free and left him standing there as she walked away. How much time had passed? And how much more would slip by until he could move? "Bye, Nic."

Behind him, he heard the rapid footfalls of sneakers hitting the sidewalk. "What's up, Cash." Jacob passed him up, burger in hand. He took a huge bite and hurried to fall in stride with Nicola. A few seconds later, she laughed, walking away with him, and Cash wanted to tear that football player apart.

The friend zone fucking sucked.

He checked his phone. T-minus ten hours until Nicola would walk into the TKX party with Jacob hanging all over her. Cash scrolled through his texts and typed out a message to Jaycee and Mira. *My place. 8 pm.*

"BRANDY, WILL YOU COME WITH me?" Nicola searched through her makeup bag. Everything she had was spread on her desk, everything except her new gloss, which was MIA. "Please."

"Don't have to ask me twice." Her roommate poked her head around from her closet door. "Wait. Why? Thought this was a you-and-Jacob thing."

"Not really. Besides, we haven't hung out all summer." Well, that wasn't true. She and Brandy had seen plenty of each other. But whatever. No way would she skip hanging with the football boys.

Brandy pulled another shirt out of her closet and held it for Nic. "Yes or no? That's such a lie, by the way."

"Yes." *On the shirt, but busted on everything else.* "Maybe a small lie."

"I'm not complaining, just wondering why."

Where to begin? Jacob was getting too touchy-feely. Her Cash fixation was hitting epic proportions. A combination of the two in the last few hours made her borderline nuts. "I just want some back up."

"Because Jacob's gonna make his move?" With her new shirt on, Brandy scooted her over, sharing the chair and the mirror. "That guy was crazy about you all last semester."

Nicola shrugged. "I don't know about that. But yeah, I'm thinking he might. Maybe. Really, I don't know."

Brandy scoffed. "Seriously, how does a girl not notice when every single hot guy is trying to call you his."

"Yeah, wrong. That's insane."

"If it weren't for Roman, their advances wouldn't be so damn vague."

Roman could be way overprotective, but there weren't guys lining up, vague advances or not. "No one's trying to call me anything, except for maybe a study partner."

"Jacob is." Brandy curled her eyelashes.

"Well, fine. Jacob. Maybe."

"Always saying maybe." She switched to curling the other side. "Boy's a catch. *Maybe* you should think about it."

Nicola sighed and looked out the window. "I'd go on a date or whatever. I guess."

Brandy laughed. "A date or whatever? Tall. Muscular. Popular. Funny. He might even be a NFL draft pick one day. And you're all, maybe I'll go on a date with him?"

"Maybe I would."

Brandy shook her head.

"What?" Nicola stood, smoothing her shirt and inspecting for lint or wrinkles, anything that could keep her from having to meet her friend's eyes.

"*What?* Are you kidding me? I've known you for a year, and for the entire year, I've never seen someone so blasé about every date. Every crush." She used quote fingers around crush. "Every party, mixer, function, game. Everything that going to college has to offer."

"I have not—"

"You have so. Fall semester, Michael. And that guy who worked at the Pizza Shack."

Nic shrugged, dropped back to her half of the chair, and focused far too hard on finding her lip gloss. "Both perfectly hot, perfectly fun."

"Same with spring semester and all summer." Brandy ticked off on her fingers. "Ryan, Brad, and Michael again. Basically four guys who had the balls enough to risk the Roman-Cash alpha-dog inquisition and get a yes when they asked you out."

Four guys. Even spaced over about a year. It seemed like a good ratio, not that she'd done the math on it, not that she'd said yes to any of them just because Cash was occupying her thoughts. "So what?"

They'd all been nice. The dates were fine. It wasn't like she was looking for a marriage proposal. She was looking for a decent time and a good guy. All of the guys met the qualifications—good looking, entertaining, and strong enough or dumb enough not to care about Cash and Roman. She scowled into a different makeup bag, still shuffling—finally.

She found her new bright pink gloss. Uncapping it, Nic lined her bottom lip while Brandy went on and on about how each of those guys were top-of-the-line boyfriend material.

"And then there's Cash."

His name made her choke and jerk, drawing a bright pink smudge of gloss right off her lip. Damn it.

Brandy smiled and clapped. "Ding, ding. We have a winner."

Nic's face burned so hot that no one could possibly see the pink gloss smudge. "Cash has been like my brother since I was born."

Brandy snorted. "Bull."

"And, even if I wanted something different, he doesn't see me like that."

"Lie number two. You weren't the only one in that cafeteria today, watching him almost kiss you senseless against the wall. You're lucky school hasn't started yet. Can you imagine if the SAC had been packed? That little bit of gossip would've flown fast and furious."

"What?" Maybe she hadn't imagined the heat. She shook her head. "That's ridiculous."

Brandy clucked. "That's exactly what happened. And nothing you can say changes the fact that Cash is all kinds of hot."

She wasn't going to dispute the looks factor. "He was yelling at me." So close, his lips had been inches from hers. If she'd moved forward, if she'd kissed him, she'd be lost forever, and that was just another reason why she could never hope for anything. With him, she'd be one of many.

"He can't stay away from you. He's always around."

"Because we're friends. The platonic, boring kind of friends." Cash was a million things, but not able to stay away wasn't one of them. Right? "No. Just...no."

"Yes."

Nic sat back in her chair as Brandy rose to pace. Maybe she wasn't totally wrong. "You think?"

"I can't believe it's taken over a year for this conversation to come up." Brandy put her hands on her hips. "But, yes. I think."

What were the chances that Cash Garrison would look at her as something other than Sprout, the kid he and her brother tormented, or the girl that he'd always protected?

Her phone buzzed across the desk, knocking into makeup. *Cash.*

Opening the message... *Hey, Sprout.*

She didn't read the rest. The chance was nil. She wasn't sure what Brandy was smoking or where her own head had been, but speculating about Cash was a waste of time. Her phone buzzed again, and she picked it up, just about to throw it out the window. But it was Jacob. *Be there in 5.*

"Time to get our pregame on." Nicola sighed. "Come on, there's a hottie football player who'll hit the draft soon, and he's picking us up downstairs."

CHAPTER 3

NICOLA BUMPED INTO JACOB AS she rounded the brick
corner of her dorm. "Hey. Sorry, J."

His hands clasped her waist, and not a single Cash-like
spark sizzled when he stayed there a second longer than
necessary. She took a step back, shoving her phone in her
purse. If she hadn't been staring at it, wondering what the rest
of Cash's text would say and if she should read it, she
wouldn't have been awkwardly removing herself from J's
too-friendly grip. So really, this was Cash's fault.

His eyes caught over her shoulder as she turned. "I invited
Brandy."

A second of are-you-kidding-me flashed in his eyes.
Whatever he had in mind for tonight, Nicola wanted to put
the kibosh on it quickly. Besides, it wasn't lost on her that
Brandy was one of those girls who batted her eyelashes at the
guys, turning them into Brandy-bots, who did whatever she
wanted. It was a respectable ability, and Nicola didn't doubt
for a second that Jacob's momentary disappointment would
be washed away by a glance at Brandy's cleavage.

"The more the merrier." J went for an arm around Nic, but

19

she hurried toward the parking lot, smooth enough that it wasn't a bitch move, but noticeable enough that a bitchy vibe settled in her chest. She made a mental note to chill out.

His Jeep idled in the parking lot, and Jacob opened the front and back passenger doors. Brandy jumped in the back and shut the door. Nicola went for the front door, but he held her arm. "Everything okay?"

"Yeah, of course. Why?"

His fingers slid down her skin. No rush. No excitement. Nothing. God, he was textbook hot. What the hell was wrong with her?

"You just seem off."

"What? No." Eek. That was too quick. Too obvious. She took a deep breath and let it out. "I'm just trying to get back into the swing of things. I was gone all summer. I've got this job internship thingie, we're getting a new place, and Roman and Cash don't approve." *I can't stop rambling because the only thing I can think of is that damn text message.*

Jacob touched her arm again. It should've been cute and flirty, but she shrugged out of it and reached for her seat.

"Here you go." He offered help, but she closed the door on her own. Jacob looked the part of popular athlete scorned: a little shocked, a little unsure what had just happened, but cocky enough to brush it off.

Brandy laughed from the backseat. "What the hell was that?"

"What?" Nic hissed. "Just forget it."

Laughter bubbled from her roomie again. "You looked like a meth-head party girl, all decked out but twitching and jerking every time he stepped close to you. Shit, Nic. If you really don't want that, pass him along. Catch and release."

Nicola turned in her seat, eyebrows arching but on the lookout for everyone's favorite quarterback. "Would you shut up already? Please."

Jacob got in, closed his door, and turned to Brandy in his rearview mirror. "What's that look all about?"

"Just fighting over you." She smiled as Nicola shot death rays at her. "Kidding. We're talking about fishing."

Confusion crossed his chiseled face. He looked over at Nic. "You guys pregame the pregame?"

That would've made her twitchy, party-girl antics make so much more sense. She leaned back against her seat, pressing her head into the headrest and closing her eyes. "Sadly, no."

Brandy giggled, and Jacob pulled out of the parking lot. Two minutes later, they were unloading at a row house that some of the team shared.

"See ya." Brandy was out the door and heading inside before Nic could beg her to wait up.

"You sure you're okay?" Jacob asked.

God, he was a decent guy. More than a decent guy. A serious catch. He had everything going for him. Smart enough. Handsome enough. Clean cut. She'd never seen him shaggy-haired or scruffy-faced. Not like Cash. Not that it ever made Cash look less handsome. Jacob never wore a cowboy hat. He made ball caps look good. She groaned inwardly. Another Cash comparison. Cash was always on her mind, and it was becoming pathetic.

"Yeah, I'm okay." She looked at his large hand on the console. Swallowing a hefty dose of unease, Nicola put her hand on top of his. His megawatt smile beamed, but she felt nothing. Actually, not true. The need to rip her hand back was there. It wasn't guilt. Was it? A hand hold was a total lead on. Maybe it was guilt. She had no interest in Jacob. He was her friend. Kissing him…the thought didn't appeal one way or another. Maybe all she had to do was warm up. She could use him to distract herself from Cash. So yes, guilt mixed with determination. She could do this. Spending time with Jacob wouldn't be so bad. It wasn't like she had to sleep with him. Kissing him would be all right. Right?

"Ready?" Jacob's eyes had narrowed.

"Oh, right. Sorry."

He moved his palm up, as though he were about to hold her hand. She pulled back and had to cover the reaction by reaching for the car door. "Let's go inside. Brandy on her own with the football team means trouble. For them."

Nicola jumped out as he turned off the Jeep. She shut the door on whatever he was saying, and it wasn't until he jogged to catch up with her that she heard him talking about jumpiness. Apparently, her train-wreck routine was on display in a major way. As they walked through the door, Jacob put his hand on her back.

"Double-deuce!" One of the guys greeted them. "Nicola."

From the kitchen, she heard a commotion with Brandy's voice in the thick of it. Nicola smiled at the guy who offered her a beer. "What's going on back there?"

He laughed. "Irish Car Bombs."

"Perfect." She was out of Jacob's grip and heading toward the kitchen.

Behind her, she heard the guy ask Jacob, "Roman around?"

Because where there was Nicola, there was Roman. Like she needed a chaperone. Well, maybe tonight she did. She walked into the kitchen and saw three guys and Brandy slam down their glasses. The room cheered Brandy on, and the guys wiped their mouths. True to form, Brandy, like Nicola, could throw down with the boys. Most times, Nic wanted something sweet to drink. Give her something pink and fruity any day. But tonight, tutti-fruity wasn't going to do it. "I'm in next round."

The football players drummed on the makeshift bar. Brandy gave her a look. Nic gave it right back and sidled up. Game on. Another round of Guinness was poured into glasses. A round of shots was pushed forward to each of them. Nerves spun in her stomach. She was about to jump in head first.

"Go!"

Guinness in one hand, shot in the other, she and Brandy toasted, dropped their shot glasses into the beer, and chugged it down, leaning forward to keep the foam from spilling on their clothes. The guys slammed down their glasses. Seconds later, she and Brandy did the same.

Whoa.

Her head spun with the rush. Her stomach felt at capacity, and she'd just started. She breathed out, giggled as she checked her mouth for any foam and looked up to find Jacob leaning against the wall, arms crossed and uncertainty on his face. Well, hell. She didn't know if he was proud she could down the drink like a dude or concerned that she just had. She smiled. He smiled. She nodded him over. This would be a good night. If nothing else, she needed the distraction.

"Who wants another?"

Brandy stepped back. "I'm out. I need a breather."

Jacob stepped into Brandy's spot and put his hand on Nic's back. Shit. She wanted to step back with Brandy. She *really* wanted to call Cash or at least text him and see where he was. She cringed inwardly. He was probably with Mira and Jaycee. Or whoever else. And there was that text she'd ignored.

His fingers flexed against her shirt. His fingertips urged her away from the bar. "Want to—"

"I'm in." She just couldn't handle it. Taking her mind off Cash needed a little more fuel before she could really let go. She definitely needed a distraction before she saw him later that night. Nicola pulled her phone out and deleted Cash's last text without reading it. That was a good step. She looked at J who seemed as if he was weighing the opportunities, possibilities, and maybe even repercussions of letting her get a little too shitty before she showed up on his arm at Roman's party. She had to nip that look ASAP. "Jacob's in too, and he needs to catch up."

Plan formed: get them both a little buzzed. Maybe she'd relax. Maybe he wouldn't notice her distraction. Maybe she could forget about the real reason she was on his arm.

AFTER THREE IRISH CAR BOMBS deep on an empty stomach, Nicola was relaxed and hanging on to Jacob's arm, laughing and joking and believing that her plan was a total

24

success. Jacob seemed not to notice her near obsessive phone checking. *No calls or texts from Cash.* She wondered what that last text had said…but tried to forget about it. She deleted it without responding, so why would Cash try again?

Focus on J. She was giving the guy a break, trying not to be so standoffish, even going as far as stepping into a conversation that some half-dressed hussy was having with him. If he was going to be her date for the night, she should at least try to act like it. Right?

She giggled to herself because, really, she was more interested in sending the girl on her way than she was hanging out in a conversation with J. Yup, total bitch move. Total buzzed bitch move. She was cock-blocking her date, who she didn't want, from flirting with another girl, who she didn't care about, more or less because she didn't like the girl's outfit. The Car Bombs had gone to her head.

They strolled through the front door of the TKX house, and she took in the scene. Fraternity rush was coming up fast, and the place was packed with the guys, the guys who wanted to be bros with her boys, and a decent sampling of random cliques: the football players, the sorority girls, the party girls, and a few guys that should've graduated college years before.

"Double-deuce." Someone from somewhere called, but the crowd had tucked Nicola behind Jacob, and she couldn't see around him. Brandy sandwiched in close to her as they pushed in.

"Three beers," Jacob answered whoever it was. He was doing a decent job at handling her as a date and Brandy as her sidekick. The more J had to drink, the more he got into the idea that both Brandy and Nicola were his dates. It worked to Nic's advantage.

Within minutes, they were on the back deck, red Solo cups in hand and people watching. *Ha.* She was people *searching.*

Roman should've been there somewhere, and where there was Roman, there was Cash. Her buzzing little heart wanted to see him. The more she sipped keg beer, the more she planned to abandon her plan to drink herself into a crush on Jacob. But to be fair, the more he had to drink, the less interested in her he seemed. Her lack of attention and interest probably fed into that.

"You girls good for a minute?" Jacob eyed them both. "I need to catch up with someone real quick."

"Yeah, yeah. We're good." Nic nodded too much. She blamed her lack of subtlety on the alcohol.

Hannah, their third roomie, walked up. "Hey! I'm back!"

Nic hadn't known she was back on campus. "Hey you!"

"Hey!" A couple of hugs later, the three of them leaned on the deck railing. "Couldn't miss a TKX party. I'll crash somewhere tonight and figure out how to pull my deposit. I can't believe we're moving in together."

"Stay with us tonight." Brandy shifted. "I have to pee."

Hannah took a sip, then said, "I'll go with you."

"I'll stay here." Nicola studied the crowd.

Hannah turned to her. "Why?"

Brandy rolled her eyes. "It's going to be an interesting semester. Let's go."

Whatever. Five bucks said that Brandy would give Hannah some drunken explanation of the conversation they'd had earlier, and Hannah had a habit of mama bearing everyone. Any interest in Cash would get Nicola mama beared, no questions asked. She sighed, almost slumping in on herself.

"Nicola." Roman's voice came from the opposite direction. She spun.

"Easy there, kid. Liable to spill the brew."

Her eyes checked his left, right. No Cash. The disappointment was stunning. It had to be the booze because she was almost in tears.

"Come on now. There's always more where that came from." Roman nodded over his shoulder. "We're on a mission to float all those kegs, but you got a bit."

Nic lifted her beer, painting on a fake smile. "Lookin' good tonight."

"Always do."

So Roman. So cocky. He was a handsome guy. She had to give him that. "Where's—"

"Matthews!" Roman saw someone over her shoulder and pecked her cheek. "Gotta give a little hell. Find me later."

Right. And now she was alone on the deck again, avoiding the alcohol-brave stares of freshmen boys. She glanced back into the house, wishing—

The familiar slide of Cash's arm and the smell of soap paralyzed her thoughts.

"You look…" Breath hot, he whispered one word slower than the next, his lips a fraction away from the shell of her ear. "Gorgeous."

A full body shiver started at her neck and ran south. "Hey, Cash." She took a deep breath and let it out slowly, letting her eyes roam over him. "Bet you'll break a few hearts tonight."

He locked her in tighter. His breath was kissed by bourbon, and the scruff on his cheeks rasped against her skin. "Nah. Not in the mood."

"The female population on campus is both relieved and saddened."

"Oh yeah?" He pulled back an inch, then spun her into a loose hug, facing him. "Why's that?"

"'Cause there's still a chance, but it's not tonight."

A lazy smile curled. "Oh, you're cute, Nic."

God, he was gorgeous. Would his mouth taste like liquor? Her plan to get buzzed had not inoculated her against his dangerous good looks and charm. Her mind raced. "So I've been told."

"What, by your *date*?" Cash tilted his head. He stepped back, dragging his arm off her neck, letting his hand smooth down her bare shoulder. His fingers drifted to her elbow. Another step, and he stuck his thumbs in his jeans pockets. His blue gaze smoldered. His button-down shirt, a little wrinkled, untucked and unbuttoned at the collar, was rolled up on his arms.

"I'm sure J's said something like that tonight. Jaycee and Mira tell you their plans for you tonight?"

"Could not care even a little bit."

She still felt where his fingers had traveled on her skin. Wanting that feeling again was driving her to distraction. Her eyes raked over his chest, sliding up to his face. He studied her. Intently. In an unnerving way, she could almost feel it. She swallowed and stole her eyes away because it was all in her head.

28

Cash stepped forward. "Let's get out of here."

His voice graveled. It had texture. She felt each word as it coated over her senses. Why did everything out of his mouth seem so much heavier? "I just got here, Cash."

"Me too."

"I didn't come by myself." Jacob was wandering around somewhere. Though she didn't care.

"Neither did I."

The air was thick. Tense. So much was unsaid. So much anticipation. She could taste it, feel it. Her heart raced; her pulse pounded. If she could touch him, hold onto his muscled arms, crawl onto his crazy-wide chest, if his arms could wrap around her and she could drown in his scent—

"What are you two so serious over?" Roman startled her.

One second. Two… What to say when she couldn't think?

"Nic's not feeling good," Cash offered. A challenge danced in his eyes.

Roman's protective gaze sliced to hers. "You're not? What's wrong?"

She swallowed at Cash's lie, and now the ball of sexual-tension-meets-too-many-drinks was in her court. Was she misreading all of this? So much could go wrong. Two decades of friendship down the drain, not to mention Roman would kill Cash. "Car Bombs. I should've known better."

Jacob joined them, holding a plastic cup, foam slipping out the top. "Another beer, Nic? Gentlemen."

Cash watched her, his gaze burning hotter than the summer sunburn on her shoulders, but she stared at the beer Jacob held. It swayed and swished like an invitation she knew she would deny. Why pretend she wasn't ready the second Cash said go? How to handle Jacob though?

"Nic's not feeling so hot." Roman saved her, though he didn't know it.

Jacob's face fell as Brandy and Hannah walked up. Brandy's expression locked onto drama in a blink. She slid a look at Cash, then at Nic, and grabbed the beer Jacob had offered Nic.

Nicola painted on a weak smile. "I think I need some air."

As if Brandy had read her mind, she nudged Jacob. "We'll keep this one occupied. Get some air, Nicola."

"We're outside already, genius." Roman smirked at her.

She hazarded a glance at Cash. Damn, he was more than she could handle. If a guy could be gorgeous, he was.

"Then go for a walk. Just get out of here if you want to." Cash's eyes crinkled at the corners like he analyzed her every move. The walk was the second open invitation from him to blow the party.

Feeling guilty, she flashed a glance at Jacob. More than a few shots deep, he seemed distracted by Brandy's boobs pressed tight in her shirt. He looked torn between a sick Nic and his tight shirt inspection. Thank God.

She smoothed her shirt. "Why don't you stay here, Jacob? I'm just going to walk around the block or something."

He nodded, the alcohol revealing his appreciation more than he probably wanted it to. Roman's face pinched at Jacob, but he turned back to her. "You're not walking around all tipsy and feeling like shit. I'll—"

"I got her." Cash put his beer on the deck railing. "I'm trying to avoid—"

Jaycee and Mira elbowed into the conversation, giggling and plastered. Hannah and Brandy rolled their eyes.

Cash nodded to Jacob. "Double-deuce. Think you can make sure these lovely ladies have a good time tonight?"

Jacob looked at Nic. She nodded, putting a hand on her stomach. *Seriously?* She wasn't even sick, and her subconscious was throwing down some so-so acting skills.

"Ladies, take care of him," Cash urged them on.

Jacob smiled, Brandy grumbled, and Hannah turned her attention to Roman. Jaycee and Mira complied with Cash's request and turned their over-the-top attention to J. Nic would've shaken her head if it hadn't been exactly what she needed.

"Nicola?" Cash drawled, pulling her to him.

Her fingers ached to touch the scruff on his cheeks. Heart pounding, she was dizzy over what was playing between them.

Roman slapped Cash on the back. "Thanks, buddy."

"No prob." Cash's chin barely lifted in response. His eyes still locked on her.

Slow and calculating, he laid his arm around her neck. It wasn't a big deal. Never had been a big deal. No one noticed. The guy had been touchy-touchy her whole life. She'd loved it, needed it, and right now, she craved it. Her mouth watered, nerves surfacing over something so mundane that no one, except maybe Brandy, had a clue.

When he guided her away from their tight circle, letting his hand slip to the small of her back, her stomach flipped, fell, bottomed out, and soared high into her throat.

Cash bent low, lips pressing into her hair. "Let's go, Nicola. We're getting out of here."

CHAPTER 4

WHEN NICOLA WORE HEELS, CASH'S mind went from distracted to just plain dumb. Tonight, he blamed her shoes. He could survive the flip-flops, the Chucks, or her Uggs. But the heels? Coupled with that little skirt that swished around her ass? Yeah, he was a goner.

He scrubbed his face with his hand. Whatever was bouncing around in his head was a big headache of trouble. When he said they should ditch that party, he'd given her an out, and she hadn't backed down. Shit, and now he couldn't ignore their...*problem* anymore.

Hell with calling *it* a problem. Whatever *it* was, it was burning red hot. Smokin' to the point of combustion. Touch it, and it was a promise to get burned, but run from it, and he'd regret it. Forever.

Line in the sand drawn. Crossing it meant major repercussions. Did he want all of that? He rubbed the back of his neck, still thinking about the swish-swish of her skirt and how she felt under his arm right now.

The only thing he knew was that Nicola's cute ass needed serious distance from Jacob and every other red-blooded male, away from anyone else who dared look at her the way he did. His stomach dropped. Fuck, man. This was deep.

They had left the house without a word and were still walking blocks later without a sound from her. They weren't heading toward campus and not really toward his place either. Not that he wanted to bring her there. Or he did... But if he did... God. What did he want?

"Nicola." He stopped, swinging her in front of him.

Beautiful chocolate eyes blinked up at him. Blonde hair framed a face that he'd memorized long ago. What he wouldn't do to drag his knuckles down her cheek to see if she was thinking anything like what he was thinking.

Cash swallowed. He'd never had an awkward moment around Nicola. Right now wasn't awkward. It was epic.

Something major could happen. Should happen.

His chest felt heavy. "Nic..."

She looked through her flutter of long lashes. He could see the rise and fall of her breasts under a shirt that flowed over her curves. His hands ran slowly on her back, down her arms, somehow finding themselves draped over her again. He pushed a few strands of hair off her cheek.

Her simple softness damn near stole his breath, and her pink lips curved and called out for a kiss. Pulling her closer, feeling her melt, Cash shut his eyes, savoring the seconds. His heart slammed in his chest. Her little breaths were audible. The warmth of her lips neared his and—

She pulled back, taking a lungful of air. Her cheeks were flushed. A little gasp passed the lips he could almost taste, and she fumbled as she whispered, "We signed on that little house."

Right. He rolled his lips into his mouth and scaled back. They weren't going there. *Okay...*

And that made sense. This was Nicola. He, *Roman*, and Nic were inseparable friends. No sense in changing that, and Roman would kick his ass for even thinking about it. But goddamn, his heart fucking hurt, and it was the first time he'd ever realized just how lost he was in her.

"So." Something he could only call sadness—or maybe disappointment—crushed his chest. He cleared his throat. "We'll get you guys moved over whenever."

"Okay." She bit her bottom lip. "I talked to my folks today. They seem cool enough about it. Moving and all."

He nodded. She probably didn't go a day without talking to her mom. That wasn't news. Nic was passing time. Trying to talk away the moment where he'd almost kissed her, where she'd almost kissed him too.

"Cash?"

He took a step closer. "Yeah?"

Her mouth opened again, but nothing else came out. Whatever it was, it wasn't *walk away, don't kiss me.*

That bit of silence was all he needed. No way was he giving up. He just needed a plan.

Nicola shifted in her heels. "And... I got that internship I was hoping for. It's the only one I could find that let me earn credit for a business class and do some translating." She tilted her head. "I know. I'm a nerd. But I own it."

That made him smile. She didn't have to work, the girl was a genius. She'd won a full ride to school and always talked about getting more experience. Gorgeous and smart. Yet another reason that Cash was crazy about her. Nothing could stop a woman with that much talent and that much heart.

But he didn't say anything, and she looked back toward where they'd come. "Maybe I should head back."

"No." Hell no would've been better. "Just…" He had nothing. "I'm glad you got that job."

"Thanks." She sighed. "I need to go. I'll talk to you tomorrow."

She walked toward the house, those people, and that party. Toward everything he couldn't've cared less about, and he wanted her to stop, to come back, or at least go home. "Glad you're spending your time on something besides football players."

She looked over her shoulder and smirked. He threw his hands up with a forced smile. "Don't be mad. Just sayin'."

"Night, Cash." She rolled her eyes then powered forward, leaving him to chase her.

He did. It took long strides to wrap hands around her shoulders and let them skim down her back. "Nic. Wait."

He stepped next to her, leaving one hand round her waist, letting it drift dangerously close to the insane swell of her ass. She slammed to a stop, leaving them side-by-side. Dangerously close. He'd been too close. Damn… He felt her in his chest.

Hands on her hips, she bounced between irritated and adorable. "You're jealous of Jacob?"

"Hell no." Well, yeah. Of course he was. "I just don't like that goon hanging on you."

"He's our friend, and he's harmless, *and* Roman's the one that I'm supposed to deal with about guys. Not you."

"Double-deuce is harmless, my ass. Dude has a thing for you, has for forever."

"That's crazy talk." Irritation colored her sigh. "He's just a friend."

"A friend on a mission to change his status."

"Cash…" She looked away.

"You never seem to know when a guy's into you…" He paused in the warm summer night then pushed. "Jacob thinks now is the right time to make his move. But more importantly, what do you think?"

Her head dropped back, and she stared at the sky. "I think…too much is at stake. His friendship means too much to me."

"You're not *that* good of friends with him."

"Exactly." Nicola fidgeted, smoothing her shirt.

What to say to that. Was it an opening? Or a 'don't go there'? Cash drew a deep breath. "Let's go for a ride."

"First a walk, then a ride."

"You ready to go home?" *Alone…* Because he sure wasn't. "Truck's around the corner, down the block."

She didn't say anything. It wasn't a no. Cash took her hand in his. He'd done it a million times for so long. Years of touching and hugging on her, teasing and throwing her around, arm around her shoulder, arm around her waist, a hand hold or an elbow grab. That had all happened, but this was different.

He rubbed his thumb over the ridges of her knuckles. He could tell she was holding her breath, and that was fine because he wasn't breathing either. He took one deep breath in and laced his fingers with hers. Locked together.

Nicola's fingers were delicate. With a gentle tug, he started toward his truck, and she fell into step. The slightest squeeze of her hand stole his heart. Cash focused on his truck. Figuring out where to go and what to do was secondary because, if he stopped now, something stupid would fall out of his mouth, like *come home with me.*

"Cash." She stopped, and he didn't let go. "Wait."

"Just…" *Just what? Give me a chance? Go home with me? Let me kiss you? Touch you, taste you? Just let us happen… Whatever that might be.*

A shy smile teased her lips. "Why'd you ask me to leave with you?"

His furrowed his brow. "What?"

"I'm not good at these things. I don't know what's in front of me and what's not. But I do know that you're standing here. And…"

"And?"

Her eyes sank shut, and she sighed, swayed. A breeze swirled around them. "I like that."

And God, I like you. He reeled her closer. Her softness pressed against him. "Nicola, we—"

"Cash! Cash!" a couple of girls across the street yelled. "We're headed to TKX! You promised us shots!"

Bubble burst. Gone was the fuzzy look in Nicola's eyes. The moment dissolved into the night, completely ruined. Damn.

She was bright and aware. Her smile looked painted. He wanted to throw his damn hat on the ground. "Nicola—"

Stepping back, she looked everywhere but at him. "I think you'd better take me home."

They were still connected at the hand, but not interlaced anymore—locked together like the friends they were. She swung her hand in his then let it drop.

Round one, lost to a gaggle of drunk chicks. He threw his arm around her shoulder like it was any old night, and he hadn't just held her hand, caressing her knuckles with his thumb.

Decision made: he'd have his head figured out, and she'd know everything, even though he'd never been less sure about anything in his life.

CHAPTER 5

MONDAY MORNING IN THE REAL world. Nicola leaned back in the spinny office chair and finished her apple. Day one of her awesome internship was off to a semi rock star start. She'd met her boss, Aleena, who seemed like a decent enough lady, if a little frazzled. The paperweight on her boss's desk read *Get It Done*. It memorialized Aleena's favorite catch phrase. Every time Nic asked a question, "get it done" was the simple answer.

So…she didn't know what to think about that and about the lack of other employees other than the girl who sat at the front desk. But this was the job Nicola wanted. Positive thinking.

Nicola had her computer password set, voice mail recorded, and other job stuff done. This was her first gig that didn't require a name badge or a uniform, even if they were paying her crap and using 'college credit' as an excuse. All hiccups and headaches would be ignored because this was the perfect job for her. Accounting and foreign translations? Her inner nerd squealed.

She opened the first spreadsheet and an ugly green folder

of bank transfers and inventory lists, all in Italian. She took a long sip of her water and dug in, matching accounts to merchandise sold.

Thirty minutes later, her phone startled her, and she grabbed it. "Nicola Hart."

"What are you doing, sweetheart?"

An instant heat flooded her cheeks. Almost kissing Cash Friday night had occupied her thoughts since he'd dropped her back at Miller Hall. She covered her mouth with her hand, whispering into the phone, "Why are you calling me at work?"

He chuckled, and her tummy fluttered. "I haven't talked to you in days and thought it might be fun to call you at work."

She looked around, worried a personal call would get her in trouble. But she'd hear footsteps if anyone walked down the hall from the warehouse or came through the front door. For the size of the facility, she hardly ever saw anyone. "How'd you find this number?"

"Asked Brandy where you worked. Picked up the phone, called, then—wait for it—asked the receptionist to talk to you."

She smiled. "Why are you calling again?" If he said something like *because I missed you,* she'd fall over dead, but it was what she wanted to hear.

"You jumped out of my truck Friday night and practically ran into the dorm."

Her heart lurched into her throat. That was the truth, but she didn't think she was *that* obvious. "I, uh…"

"The line hasn't been crossed, Nic. Nothing's changed."

From her throat to the floor, her heart tumbled and

crashed. Tears burned her eyelids. It'd been a mistake. He'd been drinking, she'd been drinking, and it was an alcohol-fueled misunderstanding. "Okay."

"That is, not unless you want it to."

Heart off floor, back into her stomach, and she was a puddle of goo. "I…"

"Think it over." He laughed low. "I'll see you later, Nic."

He hung up, and she was left holding the phone, tingling and smiling and completely unsure if she should cross any line with him. She hung up and stared blankly at the screen filled with account numbers and dollar amounts.

A large man with dark hair, dark eyes, and a *really* expensive-looking suit stopped at her office door. A buyer? A client? She put on her best smile, even though he had an underground, criminal vibe to him. "Hi. Can I help you?"

A tight-lipped smile was his answer, followed by a quick "no" in a heavy Italian accent. So it was a buyer or someone in management? She wanted to say something else, to introduce herself, but it felt all wrong.

The phone rang a second later, and the man walked away. She answered, "Nicola Hart."

She sounded just as professional as before, she was sure of it, but a little nugget of hope prayed that it was Cash.

"Nicola…"

Nope, not Cash. It was her boss, Aleena, the only person who really should be calling her on this line. Unreasonable disappointment coated her thoughts.

"Nicola?" Aleena repeated her name.

Shit, she'd completely blanked. "Sorry, yes?"

41

"Did you hear anything I just said?"

"No, I'm sorry." Nic looked at the phone's LCD screen. The call wasn't even five seconds long. She couldn't have missed *that* much, but there was a sound of annoyance in Aleena's voice.

"When you're finished with the pile on your desk, I have three more for you. Try to get through them before you leave."

Wait. What? Before she left? Nicola checked her computer screen for the time. She was supposed to be off by one because, once school started back, she had class. It was after ten AM now. That amount of work was impossible. Even if she wasn't a perfectionist, it was absolutely impossible. "Um, I don't think I have time—"

"Trust me, it will all line up. Just make sure the account names and items match up, and process the bank transfers."

Bank transfers? "I thought I was checking for inaccuracies, not moving mon—"

"Please match the names and punch them into the system. I don't need an audit. I need an *intern* to push the paper through. Think of it like busy work but in the real world. You're helping me with the workload that I don't have enough time to do."

Nicola scowled at the phone. *Intern* was said with more disdain than she appreciated, and she was one hundred percent certain that her boss didn't speak nearly as many, or maybe even any, of the foreign languages Nic did. Her boss was also one of those people who was nice in person and shitty on the phone. Probably via email too. *Great.*

She looked at her stack of paper, ready to articulate her

argument, even volunteer to bring it home with her to make sure it was done right, but the line went dead. Hung up on without even so much as a goodbye. Awesome…

———————————

CASH TOSSED HIS CELL PHONE back and forth after talking to Nicola and walked into the SAC. Before talking to her, he'd been on his way to grab a breakfast burrito after buying a new textbook from the campus bookstore. But now he had excess energy to burn. He bypassed the cafeteria, bee-lining instead for the gym but stopped. Jeans wouldn't work, even if he did want to beat the hell out of a heavy bag or run until his legs gave out. Abandoning his gym plan, he turned back around, anxious to calm his thoughts. His goal hadn't been to make Nic tongue-tied over the phone. Actually, he hadn't had a goal. Just wanted to—

"Cash." Jacob called from behind him.

Did that guy live in the SAC? Cash turned toward the voice but wasn't in the mood for small talk. He'd say hey then hoof it to camp out at the library. School hadn't started yet, and he didn't have anything to study, but no way would Jacob follow him in there. "Double-deuce."

Jacob nodded a goodbye to someone else on the team then headed his way. "How's Nicola?"

Cash mumbled, "None of your damn business," and booked it for the doors.

"She's not answering her phone, and I'm trying to track her down."

"What?" His brows arched. The guy was pushing buttons Cash didn't even know he had. "Why?"

"Think I'm going to take her out this week, trying to see what she's up to."

Cash glared and slammed the door open. His irritation level nearly red-lined. "Don't bother."

"Damn, man. If it's not Roman lately, it's you."

"What?"

"You guys can back off her already. She's a grown woman."

Cash sawed his teeth together. "Maybe Roman's issue is less about her and more about you."

"Guess all that matters is what she thinks. Dick." Jacob laughed and slapped Cash on the back. "Good thing she's had you two around. Pure as—"

Cash rounded on him, backing Jacob against the SAC ramp railing. "Finish that sentence, and I will kill you."

Jacob laughed again and threw his hands up. "Jesus, dude. Chill out." He shook his head. "Sometimes I think you're worse than Roman. The girl's my friend. I'm not going to hurt her."

No shit, he wasn't going to hurt her. Double-deuce wouldn't get anywhere near Nicola. Cash's jaw flexed, and his fists ached for wanting to shut Jacob up. "I gotta run." He ducked away before he punched his buddy. His head was mixed up, and fall semester was going to be needlessly rough if he didn't get a few things in order first. Nicola would have to speak up, Jacob would have to shut up, and he would have to man up.

CHAPTER 6

NICOLA WATCHED ROMAN HOIST THE last of her bags on his shoulder as he made his way up the sidewalk and into her new house. It was cute, like a little shotgun row home with three bedrooms, each the size of a dorm room, a real bathroom with a floor that wasn't gross, and a pool that she couldn't wait to jump into.

The sun beat down on their moving day as she sat on the tailgate of Cash's truck. She hadn't talked to him since the phone call yesterday and hadn't seen him since Friday. Today, he'd been with Roman all day while she'd been with Brandy and Hannah.

Each of the girls had packed her own stuff. The boys took turns carrying their bags and boxes out of the dorm and into the truck. Every time Nic was alone with Cash, he didn't say anything. Not a single word, but he didn't have to. He smiled. He winked. He wiggled his damn eyebrows. Basically, Cash tortured her, and she couldn't get enough of it.

Maybe it wasn't the August dog day heat that had her nearly panting. Maybe it was Cash.

Looking up at the sun, eyes closed and legs dangling off

the tailgate, she *felt* where his fingers had been interlaced with hers on Friday night, where his thumb had caressed the ridges of her knuckles.

Sighing, Nic held her fingers out in front of her and stared as though his hand had permanently stained hers. Well, it had, but the stain wasn't visible to the naked eye. The truck door slammed, and she jumped.

Cash appeared, Gatorade in hand. His jeans and t-shirt looked like heaven painted on a man. "Hey."

He sat next to her. Inches separated them, and God, she wished his leg would touch hers. Instead, he cracked the top of his drink, guzzled it to empty, and tossed it over his shoulder. The plastic bottle clattered as it landed and rolled behind them.

"For such a small room, you girls have a lot of crap." He stretched. "Still think you should have stayed put."

"Maybe." At least she'd had the illusion of a barrier between her bed and Cash Garrison with campus security manning Miller Hall's front desk. Right now, there was a serious worry that she'd grab him by the belt loops, drag him to her room—where she didn't even have a mattress yet—and jump him. That'd be embarrassing. "I like the freedom."

He shook his head, groaning. "Shit, Sprout. I—"

"Stop with the Spr—"

"Two decades of calling you that. It's habit."

"Some bad habits need to die."

"Won't happen again." His hand patted right above her knee, and her lungs skipped a breath. Maybe two. "I promise."

Brandy bounced out the front door, putting a hard stop to the adrenaline-estrogen rush that pulsed in Nic's veins. "FYI, ya'll. J's on his way over."

Cash grumbled, taking his hand off her leg. His phone rang. After a glance at it, he looked at her sideways, rolled to his side, all lazy and cute, then pushed off the tailgate. "Mira, what's up?"

Mira? Fine. *Go away, Cash.* Far, far away because she wanted nothing to do with that skank. He didn't have to take her call, just like she didn't have to pay attention to him. Or to Jacob. But still, she watched him talk on the phone, annoyed that Mira still existed. What was he saying, anyway?

He laughed, and it felt like a gut shot but also a reality check. Cash was Cash. And liking him, flirting with him, maybe even kissing him, wouldn't change the fact that he was the opposite of a safe bet in the guy department.

She let her eyes drift over those jeans and how they curved over his backside. Good Lord, he'd be gorgeous naked. And he'd be a killer in bed; she just knew it. Not that she had a ton of experience to compare it too.

Her stomach dropped. Oh, if she did end up in bed with him, she'd be contending with the memory of a Jaycee-Mira tag team, and that wasn't something she could compete with. The comparison would result in humiliation. As hot and worked up as he made her feel, she was writing a flirtatious check that she couldn't bankroll. She was plain Jane vanilla compared to Mira and Jaycee's banana freakin' split.

Cash laughed again, making her self-doubt spiral further. *I'm a moron.* Nicola tuned Cash out and buried her face in her hands. She heard footsteps, peeked through her fingers, and saw Roman's shoes.

"What's your problem?" He bopped her on the head with a plastic water bottle.

Oh me? Nothing. I'm going to kill Cash because he likes slut puppies. But other than that...I'm crazy for him in the kind of way that I want to lick him all over. So there's that... Her cheeks flamed. "Nothing. It's hot. I'm over moving."

"You didn't move a thing."

True. She tilted her head. "But putting up with you and Cash is enough of a headache."

Roman tilted his head toward Cash. "What's he up to?"

"Talking to Tits McGee and friends."

"Leave those girls alone."

Nicola crossed her arms and would've stomped but she wasn't getting off the tailgate, not while she was still spying on Cash. "No way. They're whores."

"Whatever." He laughed. "You're just jealous."

Her stomach dropped. That was true, but no way could she let Roman know that. "What?"

"You shouldn't have left them with Jacob the other night. Not that he did anything about it. I think he's hung up on you, so watch out."

"Jacob?" She let out a huge breath. Roman was talking about J. "They can have him."

"Good." Roman leaned against the tailgate. "I don't like that dude sniffing around you anyway."

She shoved his shoulder. "No one's sniffing, jeez."

"Serious, Nic. He needs to stay far away."

"All right, already. I get it." She closed her eyes again and tried to ignore Cash, tried to ignore the way her gut was twisting. Even as she opened her eyes and saw Jacob looking for a place to park his Jeep way down the street, all she could think about was Cash.

Cash ended his call and turned around. Blue eyes locked on her eyes, and the world slammed to a halt. A barely noticeable smile crossed his lips. It wasn't a fun and flirty. Maybe it was a sad realization that what happened the other night shouldn't go anywhere. Her stomach hurt.

"You want to order pizza?" Roman was oblivious. "Cash, man. You hungry?"

He never looked at her brother. "Starved."

Roman left, announcing pizza would be there soon. Still sitting on Cash's tailgate, Nicola wanted to run from the blue eyes that held her prisoner, but she couldn't. He came at her, placed his hands on the outsides of her thighs, and she was caged in place and suddenly needing an escape hatch. So she played her only hand. "How's Mira? Good, I'm sure."

"Forget about her." He chuckled. "I'm not hiding anything from you. As a matter of fact, I'm making a point not to."

"Why?" God, Mira made her want to scream. "I don't give a damn."

"Well, I do."

She balked, incredulous. "Give a damn?"

He nodded. "About what you think and how you feel."

"You're my friend, Cash. Of course you give a damn, jackass."

"And you're missing my point and irritating the piss out of me."

Nicola rolled her eyes. "That's what I do best."

49

"Oh, sweetheart. I give a damn, and you don't know what to make of it."

"I..."

"Everywhere I look." He bent close. The scent of his shampoo teased her. His breath tickled her ear lobe. "Everything I see, I think about you." He pulled back and slid his hands up her thighs, clasping her hips, lingering, then he lifted her off the truck and closed the tailgate. "And I don't know what to do about that."

Everything tingled. Her legs felt weak, and her tongue tied itself in knots. "I..."

Can't think around you. I'm dizzy. Wobbly, woozy, and would die to stay in your arms.

"Don't go silent on me now, Nic. We haven't crossed over the line from friends to.... Everything is still the same." He blew out a long breath and laughed quietly. "We can't just stay out here. Roman's going to put pineapple on the pizza if we don't stop him."

He waited expectedly, but she offered nothing. He nodded and took off.

Nic couldn't make her legs work. It was as if her flip-flops had melted into the sidewalk. "Cash."

He stopped with his back to her. He dropped his head back, shook it once, then turned around. "You made a damn good point as to why you and Double-deuce shouldn't date. It'll mess up everything. Every time we dance around the issue of us, I say something, and you say nothing."

Us... Holy shit. She stood, still silent, fidgeting with the hem of her shirt and at a complete loss for what her next move was. Just another reason that Mira should be here because that girl was never without a witty comment, even if they were all hookerific.

He crossed his arms, studying her. "You know where I stand, can guess what I want. Next move is all yours."

"Mine? Um, I…" Things were already changing, crossed line or not, and she hurt inside. Uncertainty was awful and self-doubt even worse. And what he wanted? Not a stinking clue. What—he wanted to kiss her? Screw her? Her heart jumped—hold her? A million thoughts and not one verbalized. Colossal fail.

His half-grin looked almost sad. "Right. Catch ya inside."

Sadness choked her. Doubt laughed in her head. She looked away. Jacob walked up. He held a bright pink bag with pink tissue paper sticking out the top.

"Housewarming gift. Kinda." He offered her the explosion of pink.

She took the offered bag. "You didn't have to do that."

When she looked inside, she had to laugh. Tums, a ginger ale, and a bottle of Advil.

"I shouldn't have let you do the Car Bombs. Sorry you felt like shit and had to go on Friday." He shifted. "There's a candle in there too. I didn't know what a good housewarming gift would be, but Google said a candle. So… It's a candle."

She giggled. He'd thought about it enough to Google. The whole thing was very thoughtful. Not that it made her the least bit interested in him, but it was seriously sweet. "Thanks, J."

His eyes drifted toward the house. She followed his gaze. Cash. Arms crossed. Glaring. *Great.*

Jacob waved hey and turned back to her. "Dude's been in

a seriously bad mood since he's been back. Maybe you say something to him, see if he calms the eff down."

Where to even begin?

GUT-CHECKED AND READY TO rumble, Cash walked back inside Nicola's new place, needing something to do. Now. Before he physically removed her from the reach of any guy, anywhere, but most particularly Jacob. The territorial-possessive thing drove Cash mad, and his patience was dangerously close to making him pull a couple big asshole moves.

Jacob and Nic walked through the door. Her eyes searched Cash's out, but he wouldn't hold her gaze. He couldn't. One wrong move from either of them, and he'd lose control. She dropped a pink bag by the door. It sat there, obtrusive and obnoxious. Seriously, Jacob brought her a present? What. The. Hell? A present? For what? *Fuckin' douchebag.*

Hannah lounged on the couch and pointed with her foot. "What's in there?"

"Nothing." Nic shrugged, looked at Jacob, and back tracked. "I mean, it's a candle. A housewarming candle."

Cash ground his molars. A candle? "Smooth move, Double-deuce."

"Figured the girls needed something…girly."

"Must be a big candle." The bag and all the pink crap paper falling out of it was a little overkill.

Nicola smiled at him, catching his eyes, and this time, he

couldn't look away. "Advil, Tums, and an apology for letting me drink too many Car Bombs Friday night when I didn't feel well."

Roman walked in the room, and Cash could only hope that his boy also gave Jacob a hard time. Because, a candle and Tums? Really? "What happened to you that night, Nic?"

Hannah's brows furrowed. "Yeah, no kidding. You came back to the dorms after me."

One of Brandy's eyebrows arched slowly until the girl looked like a comic book character. "Really?"

Nicola's eyes darted around the room. "I was worried I was going to get sick. So I made Cash wait for a little before he drove me home."

Roman and Hannah nodded like that made sense. Brandy's mouth opened, but nothing came out. And Jacob stood by the door, oblivious to the anger pouring off Cash and way too caught up in Nicola's short-shorts. Shit, that guy—

Knock. Knock.

Roman clapped his hands together. "Pizza."

"Thank God." Brandy popped off the couch and walked by, keeping her eye on Cash. As she passed, she whispered, "I'm on to you, Garrison Boy."

He shook his head and had nothing to say, nothing to share, because Nicola hadn't said a damn word since he suggested a serious redefinition of their quality time together.

CHAPTER 7

FIVE DAYS HAD PASSED SINCE Nicola had seen Cash.

No calls.

No texts.

Nothing.

Was he avoiding her? She *might've* been avoiding him and had decided to concentrate on something simple and positive. There were definite benefits to having a pool in her backyard. Sunday mornings were meant for lounging poolside with her roomies. The sun was out, and the day gorgeous. School started tomorrow, and she wanted back in the swing of things. She needed something to occupy her thoughts other than her internship, which sucked more and more each day, and the two larger-than-life men—Cash and Roman—well, three if she included Jacob. Not that he was really in her life, but he kept trying to edge his way in.

Cash was best avoided. She nodded to herself. If he locked those blue eyes on her again, she was liable to explode into a billion pieces. Plus, Roman's overprotective big brother act was wearing thin, so it'd been easy enough to not see him either.

Nic repositioned herself on her towel and took a long sip

of the sweet wine she'd been nursing. "Margaritas would've been better."

"With salt," Brandy added.

"Remind me again." Hannah turned over and grabbed the suntan lotion bottle. "Who volunteered to run to the store?" She rubbed some lotion on her shoulders and traded it for her Solo cup of wine. "Because I don't recall any takers when I suggested daiquiris."

"I'm not complaining." Nic shrugged, a bit of a wino-buzz starting. "Just sayin'."

Brandy sighed. "I *am* complaining."

"Yeah, but you're everyone's favorite bitch, Bitch." Hannah topped off their cups. "You not complaining would be weird."

"True enough." Brandy took a sip. "So who wants to guess why it took Nicola so long to get home last week?"

Nicola choked on her drink. "I already said I was sick."

Brandy laughed. "Oh-kay. I believe that."

Hannah looked at her. "You do?"

"No!" Brandy scowled. "No way in the world."

Nicola shrugged. "Fine. You caught me. I ran off with Cash and had crazy cowboy sex with him on the hood of his truck."

"What?" Hannah's eyes peeled back. "Well, it's about time."

Brandy rolled her eyes. "Fess up, for real."

"You're crazy. Nothing is happening there." Nicola shook her head.

Hannah sat up on her towel. "Oh my God. Something *is* happening there."

Nicola took another long sip of her wine. Something was, but hell if she knew what to call it or even if she'd follow through. Her mind was all over the place. "What if something happened?"

"Did it?" Brandy nearly shrieked.

"No. Yes. I don't know."

"What does that even mean?" Hannah asked.

"It means… I think we almost kissed. I think…" *Actually, I know.* "…that he wants something more than what's happening now."

Hannah leaned forward, whispering like their secret had to be kept from the rest of the world. And it did, because when Roman found out, *if* he found out, he'd be pissed. "So what's happening now?"

"Nothing. He's my best friend." That was the truth. *More or less.*

"Damn." Brandy shook her head. "Wish I had a hot as hell best friend trying to kiss me."

Hannah laughed and blew Brandy a kiss. "You do, bitch."

Nicola rolled her eyes. "I mean, you know, it's Cash."

"Super hot man-whore," Brandy said.

Nic scowled at her. "He's not a man-whore. He's just, um, popular."

Hannah snorted. "In bed."

"God, there's such a double standard." Brandy nodded. "But if it's true…"

Recalling what Cash had said, Nicola smiled faintly. "I don't think everything we've heard is true."

"Mira and Jaycee is true." Brandy scrunched her nose. "Those two are a mess, and I've seen that mess all over campus, and all over Cash."

"That's a major reason I don't want to fall for him."

Nicola sipped some of her wine. Her heart would get broken. Shattered, really. Besides, he was out of her league. "He's way out here." She lifted her hand in the air, making a slicing move, then dropped it. "And I'm way down here."

Hannah looked up, down, and then at Nic, copying her hand movements. "What the heck is all this?" To fully make her point, Hannah finished with a karate chop.

"You've already fallen for him." Brandy didn't bother to look at her after all. Her face scrunched, and she rolled her eyes.

Nicola blew out an annoyed breath. What was she trying to say? "I mean, he probably expects a trapeze act in bed, and I'm..."

"Sweet," Hannah offered.

Brandy laughed. "Vanilla."

"Nervous."

"Oblivious."

Nicola turned over. "All right you guys. Jeez."

"Maybe you just tell him," Hannah said.

"Tell him what?"

Brandy sipped her drink. "Yeah, tell him what?"

"Oh, I don't know. That was the wine talking." Hannah took another sip. "Sounded in my head like the right thing to say. Tell him...tell him that you love him."

Nicola choked.

Brandy choked.

Hannah shrugged. "I mean, you kinda do. Right?"

"Holy crap, shit just got real. I haven't had enough to drink for this convo." Brandy air-cheers-ed and made a big show of taking another swig.

"Shut up, Brandy."

She smiled. "You're pissed 'cause it's true."

Pissed because...it *might* be true. Nicola took her cup, staring into it as if it held secret answers. "Enough about him." Her phone buzzed. She snatched it lightning-quick. *Jacob.* Blowing out a sigh, she opened it. *Grab your roomies, day drinking starts...now.* Too late, they beat him to it. "J's having people over."

Brandy perked up. "Yeah?"

"Sounds like fun. I'm jumping in the shower." Hannah pushed up and headed toward the door. "Nic?"

She didn't want to see Jacob today. "Think I might take a nap or something."

"Lush." Brandy stood.

"Yeah, not quite."

"Nothing wrong with a little lush-ness in your life. Maybe you should give it a try. Loosen it up a little."

Ha. "Think I'll just stay out here."

"Whatever." Brandy went inside.

Left all alone and to her own devices, Nicola stared at her phone and wished Cash would call, not even to say anything that'd sweep her off her feet, just a normal 'hey, what's up?' She put it down and cleared her mind. *Warm summer sun and nothing to think about...*

"Hey!"

Startled, Nicola blinked into the sun, realizing she'd dozed off.

Hannah's head poked out the door. "We're leaving. You sure you don't want to come with us?"

"No. Really. I'm good." Closing her eyes again, Nic tried

to fall back asleep on her towel. It wasn't that comfortable. She turned. Her phone stared at her. She stared back at it. *Stop thinking about him.* That didn't work. It just made her a little crazier than normal. Crazier than thinking her phone was looking at her.

So… Another sip of wine to calm the crazy. Her phone still issued a drunk dial challenge. She'd had just enough wine to be invincible, or maybe an idiot. *Please ring.* She grabbed it. *Come on, ring.*

Nothing.

Scrolling through her contacts, she found his name, and her fingers itched to hit send. She could call. No reason she shouldn't. Not like she would profess her lifelong obsession. God, that'd be so stupid. Ruin everything. Her thumb hovered, but instead she typed out a text and stared hard at it as though it would tell her if this was a good idea or not.

Come on over, pool party.

Send.

Shit. Shit, shit, shit. What did that even mean anyway? There was no pool party. He was probably with Roman. They'd both show up, and she'd have to come up with some asinine reason she'd sent that text.

Her phone buzzed.

Sounds good. See ya in 10.

CHAPTER 8

TEN MINUTES? HER STOMACH JUMPED. Excited. Nervous. This was such a bad idea. She could call Roman to see where he was, what he was doing. If he mentioned the pool party, she could call Brandy and Hannah and get their asses home as quickly as possible. She'd probably have to threaten them, promise to write them each a term paper or something. Anything.

But…what if Cash came alone?

What if it was just her and him, sitting in the pool?

God, she wanted that.

The line—*their line*—had officially been called into question. Was this the move? Had she just made a move on Cash? *Oh my God...* No. This was a simple invitation. But why was she freaking out?

Because it was a loaded invitation.

She fidgeted with her bathing suit, with her hair. The passing minutes felt like forever, and she grabbed the wine, went to find her Solo cup—

Knock, knock.

Butterflies fluttered in her stomach. How did he get

SWEET GIRL

here so fast? True, his place was like a block away. But—

Knock, knock.

Bottle of wine in hand, clad only in her green bikini, Nicola walked to the door. Why did it feel like the next few seconds could change everything? She sucked in a deep breath and let it out slowly, cracking the door. "Hey."

He took a step back, his eyes dropping from her face, sweeping down and working their way back up. Slowly. Maybe she should have put some clothes on because the look on his face made her blood rush.

"Hey." He didn't smile, didn't come in, just stood there, swimming trunks in hand. But the heat in his gaze almost melted her bikini off.

She took a step back, and he ducked his head, hiding his face with the brim of a cowboy hat. He had on jeans and a t-shirt that made his shoulders look as broad as her new house. Then he looked back up, and she swallowed. Hard. There was lust in his eyes and a fight brewing on his face. Her decision had been made: this was a bad idea.

With a dry mouth and ready to die of embarrassment, she cursed silently. She should never have been left alone with her phone and a bottle of wine.

"Sorry, I meant to call you back. The girls took off to J's place. Thought it might take you longer to come over."

He shook his head, still standing on her front porch like she was a pariah, and he should run. This was all wrong. Crap, she'd messed everything up.

"Cash, I'm sorry—"

"Sorry?" His jaw flexed.

"You look like there are a thousand other places you'd rather—"

He shook his head again. "I…"

She went up on her bare toes, then rocked back. Nervous energy made her fidget. His blue eyes and lopsided grin would be her undoing. "You want to come in?"

"Hell yeah."

But he didn't move. A little breath of relief pushed past her lips. "Don't make me feel stupid. Come in already."

If, at that moment, he said anything with the word 'Sprout' in it, she planned to hit him on the head with her wine bottle. He didn't, so she opened the door wider, using the half-empty bottle as directional guide. It wasn't like he hadn't walked in and out a ton on moving day, but now he stared as if this were disaster waiting to happen. The air felt thick and unsure. He made his way into the entryway and pressed up again the wall.

She shrugged. "If you didn't want to come in, you didn't have to." Her voice was quiet and her thoughts scattered.

"It's not that."

She blinked, the wine not making anything easier. "Then what is it like?"

He took his hat off and ran his hand through his blond hair. When he looked back at her, his head tilted to the side, eyes narrowing just a hint. "You and me, let's go for a swim."

A swim. She could do that. After all, the pool had been her reason for inviting him over. Kinda. And bathing suit, check, she already had that on. She nodded, relieved when Cash took off to the bathroom without a word. She fell against the same wall that had just propped him up. A minute later, he was walking toward her, all golden tan, perfect chest, and still wearing that cowboy hat.

"Alrighty." He snagged her arm and started toward the sliding glass door. "You know, that bikini doesn't leave much to the imagination."

"You don't like it?"

"Ha." He stopped, turned, stared. Cash pinched his eyes shut and turned his head, looking out the door and to the pool. After a long second, a half grin tugged on his face. "I swear…"

He took the wine bottle out of her hand, and in one fast move, had her over his shoulder with her butt sticking up in the air.

"Whoa!" Way. Too. Tipsy for that move. "Cash!"

But he raced through the house, grabbing another bottle of wine off the counter as they passed, and they were outside before she could do anything but giggle and kick her legs.

"Hang tight." He pulled her to his chest and jumped into the shallow end of the pool.

Cool water splashed all around her, and without thinking she clung to his warm body, arching to avoid the cold and clinging tight to the muscle and mass, hard and hot. Goddamn, his body was insane.

He let her slip down his chest, and her arms hooked around his neck. Breasts pushing against him, legs wrapping around his torso, she swore to God the man groaned as he splashed-walked them toward the stairs.

He had one arm around her and two bottles of wine clanging together in the other hand. Putting the bottles on the ledge, he stopped and looked down. The world melted away.

Just her in his arms, and she was dying to know what would happen next…but wary of everything that could go wrong.

Really, she should let go. This was still a game. They were just playing. Flirting. Harmless enough. It was just Cash being Cash, smooth moves and smiles, always looking for a good time. But he let her stay against him. His fingers slid across her wet skin. She didn't move.

Hot sun warmed her back, and his chest warmed her front. Nicola's heart beat faster. She could barely breathe.

"Nicola…" He looked over her shoulder then shut his eyes, letting out a long sigh.

Cash sat them down, holding her on his lap. He grabbed the half-empty bottle of wine and took a long pull. Her heart clutched. She was driving him to drink. This was *so* bad. Her cheeks flamed, but as much as it hurt, she just couldn't drag herself away from him.

He offered the bottle to her. "Your turn."

"Very classy." She didn't sound like herself. That should've been funny. It should've been a joke. But she sounded too serious, too hurt and hopeful, too much like her dreams were spinning and shattering.

"As classy as drinking alone." One arm squeezed her tight, and her stomach flipped down, down, down.

"I wasn't drinking alone." She tried to think of what she'd been doing… "Brandy and Hannah went to J's house."

"But you didn't."

No… No, she didn't… She took the bottle from him and took a sip, then shook her head.

"Why not?"

Simple question. Simple answer. There wasn't a need for

her stomach to flip again. But, still, it did. "I wanted to talk to you instead."

His fingers caressed her wet skin, and prickles raced down her neck, her spine. "You could've called."

"I did."

"Nope. You texted. About a party." He made a point to look around, a slip of a smile stealing her heart. "You want to talk to me now?"

She bit her lip. Nothing would come to mind. She had so much to say, and all she could do was simply exist in his arms. He took the bottle from her and put it down. It scraped dully against the tile edge.

He was always in charge, always knowing the next move. Right now, he had to tell her what it was because her mind wanted to say *I don't know what to do,* but she was sure her mouth would say *kiss me, I'm begging you, please.*

He cupped her chin. His thumb slid over her cheek. With each slow move, she fell for him harder and harder, and their mouths drew closer and closer. Inches separated their first kiss. His kiss. One that she'd wanted before she knew what it was to want a man. Cash was her first dream, first crush, and fantasy.

Cash was all talk, total BS, the king of flirts. He didn't need to kiss her. Kissing her would've been illogical. They were friends.

"Cash." She tried to lie to herself. "You don't want to kiss me."

"I don't?" he asked, a sweet smile on his lips, his eyes narrowing.

Panic made her jump. She tightened in his arms, almost running out of the pool. "You don't?"

She'd been so wrong. This was all wrong. She'd never have a drink again. Wine made her believe in fairy tales—

"Oh, hell, yes. I do." He closed the distance, his lips finding hers, and the world stopped. Spun. Tilted and exploded. It was the perfect kiss, his lips brushing over hers, slow and lazy. He stilled for the longest moment, and she felt the full softness of his mouth, tasted his sweetness from the wine, all better than she'd ever imagined.

Straddling his lap, Nicola wrapped her arms around him, knocking his hat off, and he didn't stop kissing her.

Cash slid his hand up her back, into her hair, and held her close. Lips, fingers, head, all tingled in response to a kiss so intense, so consuming, she'd give herself to him, no questions asked. Anything he wanted. She was his.

Time paused while his mouth mapped hers. Finding her neck, Cash slid his tongue across her collarbone. His fingers played in her hair, down her back. Sitting in his lap, she felt all of him. The swim trunks hid nothing. Cash was turned on. She was turned on and dying for more, dying for him but so stuck in his unexpected sweetness, she'd drown before pulling away from him.

But he broke from her, his lips hovering close. Blue eyes seemed to see into her soul, and she couldn't blink.

His cowboy hat was long gone, and the sun was sinking deep into a purple-shaded sky. "I think I've waited my whole life for that."

"I don't believe you," she whispered.

"Believe it." He hooked her under the arms and let her dangle as he walked out of the pool with giant steps, splashing water as they reached the deck.

She shivered against him. "What are we doing?"

He kept walking, still holding her as though she weighed nothing. "Probably ordering pizza."

Not what she was talking about. "And then?"

Cash stopped, putting her on her feet and backing her until her backside met the sliding glass door. The cold glass made her arch into him.

"You're asking about us?"

Well, yeah. That was what she wanted to know. "I think so."

He smiled a lopsided grin. "I've never seen you unsure about anything."

He knew her so well. That was part of her attraction and her fear. "I've never kissed you before."

"You seemed unsure before." He pressed his body and his mouth against hers, so hot and hard. "This is a good thing, Nic."

He opened the door and stepped them inside. The cold air conditioning wrapped around her, and she shivered. God, she could stay there forever, so long as she remembered to breathe. Which she'd forgotten to do—

The front door shut, and she jumped in his arms.

"Where is everybody? Hello?" Roman called from around the corner. "Nic? Brandy?"

Oh shit.

Cash took a step back.

Nicola's finger went to her mouth. "Not a word."

His brow furrowed, eyes narrowed, looking altogether annoyed and unconvinced.

"No joke. I'm not ready to deal with him."

"Nic—"

Oh, God. She hadn't thought this through. Roman would flip. Hardcore. "Not yet."

"Calm down." Placing hands on her shoulders, he spun her around, then hollered to Roman, "We were outside, dude. What's going on?"

He was so damn calm, and she had to look like sex-on-the-brain. Her lips felt kiss-swollen. Guilt had to be painted across her face. Cash took it all in stride and snagged towels draped across a kitchen chair. He tossed one to her and wrapped the other around his neck.

Roman came into the room and went to the fridge. "Hey, guys."

He didn't seem to notice anything abnormal.

"Hey." Her voice sounded funny—really funny—like she'd been crawling all over Cash in the pool. Because she had. Oh shit, this was so obvious. Cash laughed in her direction, giving her a look that said *I know what you've been up to*. She'd kill him later. After she kissed him again.

"We're getting pizza," Cash offered.

Roman nodded. "Good. I'll order."

She and Cash both said, "No."

Her brother shook his head. "Fine. No pineapple. Whatever. I'm still ordering." He closed the fridge and pulled out his phone, walking toward a window. "Where are Brandy and Hannah?"

"Ran over to J's." Her voice *still* sounded funny.

"And you stayed here?" He sent a questioning look to her then to Cash.

Nicola shrugged.

Roman nodded. "Good, that dude's too interested in you."

When her brother walked in the other room to get his wallet, Cash ambled over, still pool damp. "You should know that bikini's dangerous enough to risk a throw down with Roman."

She looked down. Her nipples were far too noticeable. Cash's smile could've melted steel.

"Would you be quiet? He'll hear you."

Cash kissed her, quick but hot. Somehow, she was still standing, all by herself, when Roman walked in.

"Nic, you okay?"

Cash was on his way out. "I'm gonna change."

Roman hadn't a clue.

"Yeah. Fine." Except this time, she squeaked.

He chuckled, tilting his head. "Whatever. Long as you stay away from Double-deuce."

Ha, ha. Mission accomplished… Roman would absolutely freak.

CHAPTER 9

CASH SAT ON THE EDGE of the bathtub in wet swim trunks. He had to get himself in check before heading back out. *Sprout.* But damn, she wasn't Sprout anymore. She hadn't been Sprout for a long time. She'd been his distraction—or his fascination—the woman he wanted but couldn't touch. Wouldn't touch. Until he did. Then he couldn't stop.

He scrubbed his face, took a deep breath, and changed into his jeans and shirt. Looking into the mirror, he could almost see where she'd kissed the hell out of him. Cash rolled his lower lip into his mouth. Holy shit, he'd do about anything to get his mouth on her again. His eyes sank, and he inhaled slowly. The places he wanted his mouth…the things he wanted. His heart pounded.

This was why he'd avoided Nicola for…forever. Because she was intoxicating. Even now, he was staring into a bathroom mirror thinking about how he could have her beneath him. How he could've had her in the pool, in her room, on the floor, against the wall. *Fuck.* He rubbed his face again.

"Get it together." He growled at his reflection then threw open the bathroom door and headed back to the kitchen.

Nic and Roman sat at the kitchen table. She seemed engrossed in their conversation and did not look at him.

"What's up?" He let his gaze drift over her. Damn…

Roman turned his head. "Nic's explaining her new job. Something about tracking piles of money from one pot to the next in other countries. *She's* very excited."

She smirked at him. "No. What I was saying was—"

"Girl thinks she's a detective."

Cash watched her face scrunch. "Staying out of it."

"No one asked you, Cash," she said.

He shook his head and winked at her, real quick, real on the sly, and real sure Roman wouldn't see because that was better than grabbing her and pulling her against him. He'd gone from having it bad for her but surviving to having a taste and losing his damn mind.

Roman turned in his chair. "When'd you get here, anyway?"

Nic froze in place, mouth open like she had something to say but was stuck.

Her visible panic made Cash laugh. "Swung by. I was bored, wanted to go for a swim, and forced Nic to hang with me."

"What's with the wine?"

Nic remained frozen, but her jaw dropped. He was getting a serious kick out of this. "Yeah, Nic, why were you drinking by yourself?" He was gonna get hell for that and couldn't wait. His smile was as broad as her eyes went wide.

One long second ticked by. Nicola's mouth shut, and the girl glared. Hard. "Brandy, Hannah, and I toasted our new house before they went to Jacob's."

"Cool." Roman nodded and turned back to Cash. "Thought you were headed to see Mira or somebody today."

Well, fuck me. The temperature of the room could've dropped fifty degrees with the stare Nicola leveled on him. "Nah."

"Mira, huh?" She pounced. "She's *special.*"

Was that a jealous Nicola Hart? "Ignore Roman's big mouth, and forget her. Nothing there to give the girl a hard time about."

She rolled her eyes. "I'm going to change into dry clothes."

The doorbell rang as Nicola passed him, letting her bare shoulder breeze by his bicep. That was on purpose, and that was the playful, flirting Nic, even if she was scared to admit it.

"Get the pizza, Roman," she called over her shoulder, giving Cash a look as she headed down the hall.

Devious. And he liked it. God, he was going to get hard again just thinking about her testing their limits.

Roman pushed out of his chair to answer the door, and Cash waited long enough to think *don't do it,* then followed after Nicola. Her door was shut, and he knocked quietly, walking in before she could say go away.

Her hands were behind her neck untying the knot. Nic's cheeks pinked, and if he'd had better timing, that bikini top would've been gone. He advanced. "You should've known I'd be back here after you looked at me like that."

Her mouth gaped, still surprised. "Like what?"

"Like you don't really want to keep things from Roman. Turn around."

Her arms came down, leaving the top tied. She turned, and he stepped closer. Her ass pressed against him, and his hands splayed over her stomach then drifted to her side. He held her waist, letting his fingers massage deep into her flesh. She sighed. The sweet sound did something unimaginable to him. When her head dipped back, leaning against his chest, he smoothed his palms over her forearms and up her biceps, feeling the pinpricks that erupted on her skin.

"Years of wondering if that would happen…"

Her eyes caught his. "What would happen?"

"Touching you. And seeing this." He skimmed his fingers to the nape of her neck and rested on the knot of the bathing suit top. His mouth trailed by her ear. "Goosebumps, hard nipples, and breaths as shallow and as quick as mine."

His chest pounded, and she trembled against him. Aching to get her top off, he tried to remind himself why the timing was god awful. A quick shot at her goods during the time it took Roman to pay for pizza would be a travesty. He needed time, and he wasn't sure he could stop.

"Cash?" So quiet it almost killed him.

He untied the knot, but kept the strings together. Leaning over, he brushed his lips over the top of her ear, down to behind the lobe. "Spend the night with me tomorrow. No one else will be home. Just the two of us."

She nodded, and he spun her around slowly, keeping his hand on the back of her neck. He took her hand, brought it to where he held up her top, then switched their hands. It might be one of his greatest regrets, delaying the satisfaction of stripping her down.

She looked at her closed door. "We're going to get caught."

"Right now, you're the only who cares."

"Cash..."

"I'll see you tomorrow night."

Her head tilted. "You're not staying for pizza?"

"Can't do it, girl. Not if you don't want Roman to know. I can't keep my hands off you."

She blushed, and he loved it. Something primal and possessive made him feel invincible. He'd tell Roman. He'd tell the world. Right about now, nothing would keep him quiet. A quick kiss of her lips, and he was out the door. Roman was on the couch, housing the pizza and surfing the television.

"Where's Nic?"

"Don't know." Cash grabbed a slice of pizza, heading for the front door. "I forgot. Can't go to Brotherhood tomorrow night."

Roman's forehead pinched. "Dude, you have to. That's the last thing before Rush."

At this point in time, Cash had never cared less about rush week. "I'm sure you guys can camp and drink beers without me."

"Pussy." Roman went back to surfing the TV. Brandy and Hannah walked in, a shade close to hammered. Roman pointed at them with a slice of pizza, and Cash laughed at their stumbling asses. "And that's the reason I don't want Nic hanging with Double-deuce."

"Roman!" they called, all drunk and annoying.

Cash used it as an escape plan and tried to ditch out before Roman noticed.

"Cash," Roman yelled over the drunken babble.

So his grand escape plan didn't work. He turned at the door. "Yeah?"

"Thanks for keeping our girl safe and away from pieces of shit who do this to them." Roman motioned to Hannah and Brandy, who flopped on the couch together, giggling on their way to passing out.

"Right." And now he felt like the piece of shit because he'd been mauling his best bud's little sister. Roman expected Cash to keep his paws off her and protect her. He wasn't sure exactly what Roman wanted, but if he could've had Nic bubble wrapped, he would have. Shit, maybe this was more complicated than he'd thought. Nicola was right. Keep mum until… He had no good answer. Until later. For now.

CHAPTER 10

NICOLA WOKE UP NERVOUS. SHE sat through lunch nervous, did laundry nervous. And now she was frozen on the edge of her bed, so nervous she couldn't move. Outside her room, Brandy and Hannah tried to entice her out to the pool. They thought she was on crack for all her smiling and fidgeting, and now she had an hour until she headed over to Cash and Roman's. But Roman wouldn't be there.

Holy shit.

Her stomach flipped. Again.

This was really happening, and she couldn't tell a soul. Not yet. Until then, she'd have to hold in all the Cash-mania and be a big girl about it because tonight, she was spending the night in his arms.

Just...holy shit.

Her cell buzzed on her bed, and she looked down. *Cash.* Her perma-grin quadrupled in size when she opened the text.

All alone.

That's all it said, and it was all she needed. Roman had left for whatever frat-thing he had to do, and Cash was alone. She jumped up and gave her outfit a once over: cute summer skirt, wedge heels, simple pink shirt, casual date wear. She could get out of the house in it without an interrogation from her roomies. After a quick spin in the full-length mirror, she smoothed a nonexistent wrinkle out of her shirt.

Oh, God. She was gonna puke.

"You can do this." The reflection in the mirror wasn't sold. She could do this... Absolutely. If her nerves would just go away already.

Shit. No, she couldn't. It was too fast. Did he expect her to sleep with him? That's what she wanted: Cash, all of him. And she'd known him her whole life. It wasn't as if this was some random dude. Had anyone ever turned him down, anyway? What if she was just something he needed to work out of his system?

Nicola shook out her hair. Tying it into a ponytail, she kicked off her shoes and fell back to the bed and dropped back. She couldn't do this. Her cell rang.

Cash.

"Hi." She curled around a pillow, aching to be in his arms and terrified that all their flirtations would end in disaster. "I'm still at home."

"Why?" His voice was low, tinged with disappointment. It rumbled over her, a tsunami of tension, twisting her stomach.

Maybe she'd made the wrong decision about her earlier decision. This was confusing, and then self-doubt crept in. "I..."

"Nicola—"

"Cash, look." She closed her eyes and pretended what was in her head was safe to say. "It's dangerous to want somebody as much as I want you." She took a deep breath, not believing she'd said that aloud. "And it's scary that I've never kept anything from you except how I felt about us, and I don't want to keep that hidden away anymore. But I don't want to ruin, ya know, everything."

Cash was silent. Not the greatest response.

She bit her lip. "Yesterday... That was... But today, tonight. Cash, I don't know."

"What don't you know, Nic? Cause yesterday, you knew what I knew."

"And that is?"

"That tonight you're falling asleep in my arms. Waking up the same place too."

He stole her breath. "Cash."

"Stop saying my name, and get over here. Or I'll come get you, your choice. Make it fast. I already have my keys in hand."

"I'm coming." It was like all she'd needed was to hear him say that. She was up and on her feet, slipping on the wedges and walking out the bedroom door. Phone still pressed to her ear, she shouted to Brandy and Hannah and left. She could drive, but then her car would be there.

Cash didn't say a word, but she could tell he was still on the line. He was only one block away, but the wedges weren't the greatest idea.

"You walking over?"

"Yes."

"You want me to pick you up?"

"No." There was his place. Nothing would stop her now.

"I'd be there in a second."

"Too late, I'm here." She knocked on the door instead of barging in as usual.

He cracked it open, slowly dropping his phone into his pocket. She put hers in her purse, positive her hands were trembling while he looked all easy going.

"Knocking now, huh?" He winked. Cash was barefoot, wearing khaki shorts and a shirt that hugged every muscle in his chest. "You should come in. The neighbors might be scandalized."

"Jokes." She walked into the cool air. A million times, she'd walked into his place, but suddenly she had no idea where to go. The air crackled, heavy and slowing her thoughts. She turned, and her whole body felt awkward.

"Want to eat something?" He walked past her toward the kitchen.

She trailed the familiar path. "You want to eat?"

At the fridge, he turned around. "What, you thought I'd jump you the second you walked through my door?"

"You're not going to?"

He dropped his head, rubbed his neck, then looked at her. "Not when you're over there looking as if you've never seen me before."

Well, that's how she felt: unsure, unsteady, absurd. She knew that. But still. "I'm sorry."

"Sorry?"

"I don't know what to do or what to think." She also didn't know when to shut up because someone needed to stuff her wedges down her throat. This was bordering on embarrassing.

"Maybe I wasn't clear before." He took a step closer. "I want you. I want to kiss you. Want to tear that skirt off your sweet body." Another step closer, and he was right on her. "I want to hear you moan, and I want to watch your face."

She couldn't breathe, but her whole body flushed. As he leaned in closer, almost kissing her, that comfortable this-is-all-right warmth hugged her. She nodded. He nodded too, his lips brushing hers, his hands finding her waist and pulling her into his embrace.

Cash didn't kiss her, but he didn't take his lips away. "I want you."

She nodded.

Stepping back, he took her hand in his. "Come on, let's go."

"What? Where?"

"We're going out to dinner."

She shook her head. "No—"

"You would've gone to dinner with me a week ago, even two days ago. No one will know the difference. Come on. I'm starved."

"But... Um, okay."

He pulled her close again, wrapped his other hand around her back. "*Um, okay*? Not-uh. Go out on a date with me. Have dinner with me. And at the end of the night, come home with me. Say, 'yes, I want to,' even if you're going to make a big deal out of hiding it from Roman."

"You don't think I want to?"

He smiled. "I'm not sure you know what you want."

Her neck and cheeks heated. "Nobody in the world has ever said no to you. Why do you think I would?"

"I don't care about anyone in the world, nor am I asking them out to dinner."

"Then why are you?"

"Christ, Nicola. It's you. I want you. I've wanted you for as long as I could remember. I like you. You think I would've kissed you if I wasn't one hundred percent sure? You think wanting to have dinner with you is some pain in the ass I've suffered through over the years, every time I had a meal with you?"

She bit her lip.

"I'm about to drop some very heavy shit on you, so brace yourself." His lazy grin kicked up on one side. "You braced?"

Nope, just about the furthest thing from it, actually. "Lay it on me."

"You sure you can handle it?"

She smacked his chest. "Stop it."

He caught her hand and brought her knuckles to his lips. "I've been chasing you since before I knew what chasing a girl meant."

An instant flash of heat tore through her, but she couldn't stop smiling. "Ha."

"I'm going to change clothes, then let's go."

He stationed her on the couch and was in and out of his room, jeans and a t-shirt on within seconds. "Dinner with my secret girlfriend."

Girlfriend? "Now I'm going to call you out on that." But she followed him.

"What?" He snagged his keys off the counter.

"Girlfriend."

His eyes danced when he chuckled. "Oh, scary word."

"You don't do girlfriends. That I know."

"I never had you."

"Now there's a Cash Garrison line."

"I'm going to forget you said that." He walked them out the door and locked it. "Want to duck and hide behind the bushes? Maybe we could barrel roll to the truck like ninjas. No one would see us then. Might mess up your skirt though."

She rolled her eyes. "Don't forget, I've known you my whole life."

"Then you somehow missed the fact that I've never chased any other girl. Ever." They were at his truck, and he clicked it unlocked, opening her door. In a second, he had her lifted up and in her seat, her legs dangling out the side and his torso pressed up against her knees.

"You don't have to chase me."

"Kinda like it though. You're fun."

"Well, you caught me, so you're going to stop?" *Please don't stop.* She'd be heartbroken beyond repair.

"Not on your life, sweetheart." He pressed a kiss to her lips, then backed away, throwing his hands in the air. "I know, I know. The neighbors might tell Roman." Winking, he shut her door and jogged to the driver's side, joining her inside.

"And Roman would be pissed."

"Wouldn't be the first time. Won't be the last time." Cash started the truck and pulled out of his space. "That's how he and I are. You know that. Anyway, where we going? Seafood, Italian?"

"Shouldn't you have all that planned if this is our first date?"

He stopped the truck and looked at her, eyes narrowed, a tickle of a smile crossing his face. "You know what? You're right." He put the truck in reverse, pulled back into his spot, and threw it in park. "Give me five."

"What?"

He leaned over and kissed her. "Go with it."

"This is getting easier. Once I got past my nerves." She sighed against his mouth, wrapped her arms around his neck, and let him all but drag her into his seat.

"This?"

"Us."

His tongue teased her neck. "Us."

Her heart pounded, and her skirt wasn't covering much as his hand smoothed up her thigh. "We're never going to make it to dinner."

"To our first date," he corrected and put her back in her seat. With a long look, he jumped out with a lazy grin on his face. Whatever he had up his sleeve, he was excited about it, and she couldn't wait.

CHAPTER 11

NICOLA WATCHED CASH WALK OUT his door with a duffel bag thrown over his shoulder. He tossed it onto the bed of the truck and jumped back into the driver's seat.

"What's that?" She nodded over her shoulder.

"A date-in-a-bag." He turned a corner.

Oh, because that made sense. She peered out the back window. "Doesn't look like much, just so you know."

He flipped the radio on, blasting music as he pulled onto the highway. "I don't look like much, but you seem to like me just fine."

Ha. Cash was sun-bleached tan with a perma-trail of girls following him around campus. Liking him *just fine* was like her saying she was *just okay* with breathing.

"Where we going?" she asked as they passed exit sign after exit sign.

"Out." His smile toyed with her as he hit the gas pedal, rushing them somewhere faster than before. But every logical location was passing.

They'd blown by dozens of mile markers. Not like their college town was bustling, but they'd gone from signs of life to rolling hills and bad cell coverage. "Out where?"

"Come here." He pulled her under his arm, smelling like soap and making her dizzy with want. "We're headed to the sticks."

"The sticks? That doesn't sound very date-ish."

He touched his chin to the top of her head as she nestled against him. "But it does sound very you and me."

He exited off the highway onto a Podunk ramp with nothing listed on the sign other than a state route number. No restaurants, not even a gas station, so he wasn't kidding about the sticks.

The truck slowed as he ambled down some back country road, and she scooted from under his arm to the door and hit the window button. It rolled down as songs played on the radio about summertime nights and falling in love.

With one arm tossed over the steering wheel, he pressed his lips to her temple, squeezing her close. "You good?"

Her hair blew around her face, tickling her cheeks. "Yes." She was better than good. What was the word for that?

He pushed his window button too and cranked the radio another notch. Cruising under his arm, check that one off a bucket list she hadn't even known she had.

They cut from the state road and passed through an open gate that interrupted what looked like miles of split-rail fence. The sky was purpley-orange with splashes of red.

"Do you have a secret hideaway I didn't know about? I thought I knew everything about you."

He chuckled. "A friend of a friend owns the land. River's up ahead. Good place for a trip with the guys or…"

"Or?" *Or what?* All alone in the middle of nowhere, a million ideas popped to her mind.

He didn't answer and pulled off the rough road onto a gravel path. The truck bumbled and bounced back and forth. The sweet smell of grass and a summer's early night air floated into the truck. The river was ahead, and he pulled over toward a rough mowed area. "Or to hang with you for the night. No roommates, no cell service. Nothing but you and me."

Her stomach flipped. "And here I thought we were going to get dinner."

His perfect smile grew as he shifted into park. "We are. Come on."

There was no way in the world she was fishing. If he wanted to do that, he could've gone with Roman. Maybe she'd spent too much time being one of the guys. Maybe he thought she wanted to go hunt down her dinner and haul it back to town. Maybe he had lost his damn mind because dinner didn't look like it existed out here, but—her gaze swept—it was the most beautiful place she'd ever seen.

Rolling hills, a slip of sunlight that was rapidly disappearing, and the now giant moon hung low in the dark sky.

He opened his door, and in one smooth move, hooked his hand around her hip and pulled her out his side. She toddled in her wedges over the uneven grass, holding his hand. It was the second time today those shoes hadn't worked. They were cute, but that didn't matter much.

He popped the tailgate open, and she eyed the bag.

"Dinner's in there?"

"Are you doubting me?" With a quick lift, he put her on the tailgate. All this manhandling, picking her up, putting her down…it made her cheeks hurt from trying to hide the smile. It was like she had given him the green light the other day, and all their just-for-friends touching and toying had morphed into some kind of alpha-possessive hold that made her feel wanted.

Cash jumped into the bed and grabbed the bag, jumped off the truck, and bounded away. "Stay put."

"Leaving me to fend for myself?" She sat on her hands, watching his broad shoulders disappear into the dark.

"Hang tight, impatient."

Well, yeah, impatient. Sitting lonesome on his tailgate wasn't what she'd expected, and curiosity was killing her. All the waiting made her want to chase after him, hang in his arms, and let him hold her, kiss her, and everything else he promised, all night long.

Make you moan.

Her stomach dropped, and heat bloomed deep down.

There was a sudden burst of light in the dark distance, and Cash was illuminated by a roaring fire. Whoa, he'd made her a campfire. Grinning and kicking her legs back and forth, she watched him come back. Her shoes hung off her toes, and she kicked them off when he was a few feet away. Cash sidled up to her, pressing between her knees, and she hitched her legs around his hips.

"Your dinner awaits." An earthy campfire smell clung to him. He kissed her lips, tasting sweet like candy. Cash pulled her against his chest, lifted her off the truck, barely taking his mouth from hers.

His large hands cupped the back of her thighs, and she bear hugged him, locking her ankles behind him. He walked them toward the fire. Overhead, a million billion crystals shone in the sky.

He set her down on a blanket. "S'mores."

Her mouth gaped. For a second, she could've sworn there was a smidge of apprehension in his voice. Something in his eyes flickered like maybe he didn't know her at all, like he thought maybe she wanted a typical first-date-in-a-box. Dinner, movie, make out. But she didn't, and s'mores were her favorite.

"You had s'mores stuff at your house?"

He shrugged. "Well, yeah. I told you a month ago, or whenever, we'd make 'em. You said you wanted s'mores. I said okay."

"I can't believe you remembered."

"Ouch." Teasing, he reached for her hand and fake-grabbed his heart. "Not gonna lie, Nic. It hurts that you think I wouldn't."

"Ha. Liar."

He laughed. "Maybe. But no shit, you said you wanted s'mores, I bought s'mores stuff."

For the next fifteen minutes, she caught marshmallows on fire and handed off flaming balls of sugar. He blew them out, made her chocolate sandwiches, and she finished every one, licking the stickiness off her fingers.

When the last one was gone and her hands were wiped clean, he bagged all their trash and sat down next to her. "I gotta tell you something."

"Tell me what."

"I'm glad I never wasted something as good as a first date on some chick who would poke at a salad over dinner."

"Wait, what?" He'd never been on a date before? No way.

He pulled her between his legs and whispered into her ear. "Wait what, what?"

That didn't even make sense, but the words slid down her spine, filling her with a want so intense she bit her bottom lip. Cash trailed his lips down her earlobe and neck. She'd relaxed so much she'd forgotten she was nervous. She'd completely forgotten that she was vanilla to his usual banana split. Until that moment. Nerves skyrocketing again, she tried to remember where her mind had been. "What'd you say about a first date?"

"Never had one before." He kissed the spot where her neck turned into her shoulder, letting his tongue slide softly.

And there she went, her world clouded again, and want replaced nerves. "I don't believe you." She dropped her head back against his chest, giving him all the access he wanted. "But if you say so."

His hand roamed over her stomach, smoothing back and forth on top of her t-shirt. Such a tease, so experienced, so insanely aware of what he was doing to her, and all she could do was exist in the moment, back pressed against his chest, legs straight ahead, and skirt riding up her thighs.

"You don't have to believe me. You're the experienced one with first dates. And I hate every guy who's ever laid eyes on you." His hand dipped under her t-shirt swirling circles around her belly button. "As first dates go, how am I doing?"

She nodded. "Good."

"Just good?" He sighed against her skin then kissed. "That sounds generic, and here I thought I was being original."

Giggling, she nodded. "Great. Amazingly well. That better?"

"Getting there. I'm going for memorable."

Damn, he kept stealing her heart. "Memorable. We're there."

"Good." He bit on her neck. "'Cause I'd hate to be just another guy."

She shook her head without thinking. "No other guy could compare."

"Good answer." Cash toyed with the top of her skirt, rubbing his hands over the fabric, over her hips, pressing her back against the erection evident through his jeans.

Her stomach fluttered, and her mind spun. "Not much to compare to anyway."

"Guess Roman and I did a decent job at keeping the wolves at bay."

She nodded, noticing how breathy she felt. "Guess you did. You didn't have to though. Nothing was ever that serious, and no one ever stuck around that long."

"Sure as shit not for them trying," he grumbled.

She giggled nervously. "True." Her heart had never given anyone but Cash a chance. "I never had the same thing in mind that they did. I guess I can't blame them. Wanting something physical when I wanted…" *You.*

"Wait. Nicola." He turned her in his lap so that her legs went over his thigh.

She wriggled around, hooking her leg around him, straddling him, hands lightly lying on his shoulders. If he lay down, she'd be sitting on top of him, and she wouldn't even know what to do with herself. One second, she was on top of the world, the next, she felt gangly and awkward. Legs too long, making her feel better suited to be a jogging partner than sex-scapade participant. But still, looking into his eyes made her dizzy. "Hmm?"

Those eyes, dark with arousal but narrowed as though studying something. They made her even more nervous. One arm stayed wrapped around her back, but his other hand smoothed her hair, pushing it off her cheeks. "Are you a virgin?"

What? "No!"

Eyes wide and heart stopping, she'd just died of embarrassment right that second in his arms, yet somehow still felt alive enough to feel the awful cringe of humiliation.

"Seriously, it's not a big deal if you are."

"I'm not." *But I might as well be.* Oh my God, this was mortifying. She needed out of his lap.

Ignoring her, his hands locked her in place. "Nic?"

"Are you trying to ruin everything?"

Dead serious, he shook his head once. "Nope."

"So what then?" God, her chest was caving in. Her cheeks had never been hotter. It'd be a lot better to have this conversation far out of his reach. She tried to move again. Better not to have this conversation at all. "I need to g—"

"Why you running?"

She blew out a breath. "I'm not."

He ran his hand up her back. "Then why are you acting like it's a big deal?"

Squirming wasn't making anything better. Amusement lit his eyes.

She huffed again. "Because, you are…*you*. And I…"

"You? What?"

"I'm vanilla, and you're freakin' Baskin Robbins." Nicola closed her eyes and took a deep breath. "The only reason I've ever even had sex was because I was trying to forget about you."

There. She'd said it. Rushed and jumbled, but it was out there. She'd already warned him that she couldn't keep the truth from him anymore, and that was the big granddaddy of truths. "It's not like it's something I've done a lot, or even recently. But, no, I'm not a virgin."

All the light and laughter on his face was gone. She'd killed the mood, ruined their date night. Maybe she'd get another shot at it some other time. Hopefully, the drive home wouldn't be terribly awful and awkward. He could even drop her off in front of her house. No one would know the difference.

He dropped his head, pressing his forehead to hers. Now he pitied her. This was worse than she'd expected. Her eyes burned, and a big, huge, enormous knot resided in her aching throat.

"I'm an asshole," he whispered.

What? Had she heard that right? "Cash..."

He tipped them sideways. Startled, she landed on her side, safely held, with his bicep acting as her pillow, their legs tangled, and the fire roaring behind him.

"Whatever you think about me." His face was shadowed and sweet. "Whatever you've seen or heard, half of which I can promise you isn't true, it's because I never thought I could have the only girl I wanted. You." He kissed her slowly, working her mouth open. He paused, pulling her even tighter. "The blame lies with me, Nic, and it kills me that I didn't tell you sooner."

Heart racing, she didn't know what to say, but her stomach climbed past the knot in her throat. Lost in his sapphire stare, she felt like the universe stopped and started at her command. She opened her mouth, but nothing came out.

"I need you, sweet girl. Always have." His palm found her cheek, his thumb caressing as he kissed her.

Her body tingled, fingertips and toes, mind and soul.

He kissed her again, deepening it, and she craved him. All her hesitation was gone. Everything else was replaced by complete trust. Still on her side, her one arm was hooked around his neck, but the other found his rock hard stomach and explored over the cotton t-shirt, then under, to the ripple of abdominal muscles.

He sat up with her still in his lap, shucked off his shirt then snaked his hands up her calf, drawing a slow path as he lay them back down. His hands drifted over her thigh, and she watched him watch her.

"You okay?"

She nodded, pretty much lying because nothing about tonight stooped to the level of okay.

"Good." His fingers smoothed against her skin, massaging the inside of her thigh, teasing higher, higher, then dragging the back of his knuckles over her mound.

She couldn't breathe. "You're a tease."

Propped on his side, he loomed over her. "Yup."

"I like that."

He did it again, slowly torturing her with a touch that was barely there, spreading her legs wider. "Your little skirt's killing me."

"That was my plan."

His fingers ran under her skirt until they drifted along the edge of her panties. "But this little lace number you've got going on." Cash shook his head almost as deliberate as he stroked her. "Has to go."

She nodded, and he slid them down, slipping the lace off one foot at a time, then he kissed her ankle. His hands slid up her legs, and he kissed the back of her knee, almost bucking her off the ground with one long, warm slash of his tongue.

Cash chuckled. "Like that too?"

"Apparently." Her voice was raspy, breaths panting. He did it again. "Yes. Yes, I like that."

"Good." Pushing between her knees, he trailed a burning path of kisses higher until he stopped at the juncture between her legs. He didn't move. Didn't kiss. There was no touching or teasing or torturing for the longest second of her life, and then he kissed her.

Oh God... Her head rolled back, and she arched as Cash swirled his tongue around her, hiking her skirt high. Both his hands moved up to her hips, and his broad shoulders kept her legs wide.

"Cash." She stared into the star-covered sky, felt the warmth of the fire and heard its crackle while he did his best to kiss her to oblivion.

His tongue drifted to her opening, and the pad of his thumb began a sinful circle on her clit. He speared her with his tongue, then added his fingers. She couldn't see straight. Her eyes closed, embracing all that she could. Her body trembled, spiraling out of control. He increased his onslaught, stronger, faster, deeper, until white lights exploded behind her eyelids. She came, and the rush of satisfaction pulsing through her blood was the best she'd felt. Ever.

"Fucking beautiful." He tugged her shirt off her limp body.

Feeling as sexy as the look on his face said she was, she rested her hands on his belt. The leather worked out easily as she unbuckled, then unsnapped the top button of his jeans. His erection strained in his pants, and just the thought of Cash naked made her heart race.

Two fingers touched her chin, and he brought her gaze up. "What's going through that pretty head of yours?"

Her gaze shot to the campfire, then back. "You're gorgeous."

"Guys aren't gorgeous."

"Well, you are."

He smiled, kissed her, taking off his pants and lying next to her, entirely naked. Lord, she was right. He was gorgeous. Even in the campfire light, she could see how perfect and corded his body was, and how thick his erection stood.

Every inch of her was on fire. His mouth worked over her, his body was positioned between her legs, and she had never been so incapable of breathing yet so alive in the moment.

While he worked on a condom, her hands memorized the feel of his strong back and the sway of his muscles leading to his firm backside. Everything about him was powerful, tall, overbearing, over top of her, but completely, deliciously seductive.

"You okay?" Forearms caging her head, his fingers ran into her hair and his hard-on pressed against her opening.

Again with the okay… She nodded yes, but she wasn't actually sure. A sudden panic pounded in her chest. This was going to hurt. It had to. He was—her breath hitched as he pushed into her. Just a little bit. And a little more.

"Okay." It was a breathy, raspy whisper, but it was the truth. Her mouth hung open, her entire body trying desperately to accommodate and enjoy everything. It was pleasure mixed with a hint of pain. Or more than a hint as she walked her feet up, bending her knees and opening more to him.

"Relax."

"Relaxing." She nodded, her fingers clawing into his back. He felt so damn good. The discomfort was intoxicating. "Trying."

Cash kissed her, touching her soul and sliding deeper again. "Damn, Nic."

She tasted his neck, kissed the faintly salty taste, and smelled his soap mixed with the outdoorsy scent clinging to them. She wrapped her legs around him and hugged him for all she was worth. His forehead touched hers, lips kissing as his body pushed her faster and deeper.

This was more than she'd ever experienced, more than she ever dreamed. Lightning powered in her veins, muscles tightening. Her vision went hazy, went brilliant, did a thousand things in between. All she could feel was him. All she could think was how perfect he felt. Her muscles tightened around his shaft, gripping and building for more.

"Come for me." Low and strained, his voice rumbled, growling, ordering her to fall apart for him. "Please, sweet girl. I need it. Need you."

Cash needed her? She would've called him a liar, but his eyes locked on hers, intense and demanding. She saw nothing but raw honesty. Unable to control her reaction, she climaxed, crying out his name. Stars and sparks and sizzle flared, and he rode her deeper, holding her tighter.

His fingers dug into her. Every part of his hard body tightened as he strained, growling her name with powerful thrusts so deep she felt he touched her soul. One last long push and he stilled, groaned, coming with his jaw open and his eyes squeezed tight. "God, Nicola."

He collapsed on her, his chest heaving as hard as hers. Feeling him fall apart, watching his face, and knowing it was because of her…her heart seized.

"Cash…" He nodded, holding her tight. His fingers brushed her hair, and he murmured in her ear. *She was beautiful. She was perfect. She was his.*

Catching their breaths together, lips connected, breathing in tandem: this had to be a dream. The campfire's flames blazed high.

Cash left her to dispose of the condom, bringing back with him a second blanket. He tucked her close and she closed her eyes.

She kissed him. "Definitely memorable."

"Good."

Nicola rested her chin on his chest. "Tonight was perfect."

His golden smile warmed her from the inside out. "Best date ever."

She closed her eyes, laying her head down, and watched the flames. Cash's fingers trailed up and down her spine. Burrowed beneath the blanket, she wanted to ask him what he was thinking. Wanted to see if anything had changed. Wanted to just drift to sleep for only a minute…

CHAPTER 12

IT HAD BEEN TWO HOURS since Cash pulled up to Nic's house and kissed her goodbye. He hadn't planned to spend the night out there, but when he woke up with her in his arms, a damp dew settling over everything and the sun rising over the river, and he wouldn't have changed a thing.

Checking his watch for the millionth time, he decided a two-hour separation was long enough. He picked up a dozen donuts and headed over to Nic's place. If the girls weren't up yet, he'd get them up.

Using his fist, he bumped twice against the door before letting himself in. "Morning, ladies." He walked through the door. Nic, Brandy, and Hannah were stacked on a couch in pajamas, nursing coffees and watching television. "I bring gifts."

Hannah popped up first. "Donuts? God, you are a good man."

Brandy looked way hung-over. "Get me one, Han."

Hannah hooked two donuts. "Nic, want one?"

Cash walked toward her, offering the box. "Breakfast?"

"Yeah, sure." She blushed, and he wasn't sure why, but he liked it.

The four of them crammed onto the couch, watching whatever the girls had on, and his fingers traced over Nic's arm.

"Stop it," she mouthed.

He feigned stupid. "What?"

She elbowed him. Brandy grumbled that they were making too much noise. Hannah reached over Nicola toward the donut box at the same time he did.

"Dude, Cash, what happened to your arm?"

He looked down. Three itchier-than-shit mosquito bites stood loud and proud. "Bug bites."

Hannah took a big bite of her donut. "Nic's got some too. Where the hell have you two been lately?"

Nicola choked on her donut.

"Easy there, sweet girl." He laughed, clapping a hand onto her back. "Yeah, Nic. What have you been up to?"

Nic turned, glaring, mouthing all kinds of things that he assumed were threats. Slowly, Brandy turned her head, eyes narrowed and curious, which made Nic sit still, straight back, knees pressed together and feet flat on the floor.

"What's with you?" Brandy's evil eye bounced from Nic to Cash and back.

He chuckled. "Yeah, Nic. Something up?"

Brandy's glare tightened.

Nicola didn't look away from the TV. "I need more coffee."

Cash stood up. "Me too."

He laughed when she growled at him quietly enough that only he heard. So damn cute.

99

Roman walked through the front door, eyeing Cash. "Thought I'd find you over here. Damn, you missed quite the night." He stretched and nodded to the box of donuts. "Throw me a donut."

"There's no donut throwing in here." Hannah waved her hand a couple of times. "Watch out. Your butt's in the way of the TV."

Nic grabbed the donut. "Here." She handed it off and shuffled toward the kitchen. Cash was fast on her trail.

"Hey—"

She spun. "I am *not* ready to tell the world."

He crossed his arms and leaned back against the kitchen counter. "I could take that as a major insult."

She rolled her eyes and refilled her coffee, drowning it with milk and sugar. "But you won't."

He pushed off the counter and caged her against it. She kept her back to him. She smelled like lavender. "You took a shower."

"I slept outside." She looked over her shoulder as he pushed her hair off of her neck. "That, and I *normally* take showers."

"You smell nice." His lips slid down her skin.

Turning around, she looked over his shoulder. "If Roman comes in, he'll think you're doing the Heimlich."

"Better than kissing your neck, right?"

"I'm being serious." Her nose wrinkled as she tried to make her point, failing in an angry kitten kind of way. "Think about it. The second Roman finds out, everything changes. He won't see you as his best friend. And whatever you guys do when you hit the bars, Lord knows, bringing home whatever—"

He shook his head. "Don't be like that because it's never been like that."

"I'm just saying that everything's going to change. Can't we wait and get back into the swing of things at school? If he has something to do, he won't be so on my case. Yours either." Footsteps approached in the hall. "Please, Cash."

He took a step back, and she grabbed her coffee off the counter as Roman walked in. He went straight to the fridge and rummaged through takeout boxes.

Roman pushed a few containers around. "Don't you have anything to eat?"

"Donuts." Nicola sidestepped further away from Cash, and he ground his teeth together.

Roman abandoned the fridge, grabbed a mug, and poured a cup of coffee. After a long sip, he twisted his face. "What's wrong with this?"

Nic shrugged. "French Vanilla."

Her brother dumped it into the sink and turned to him. "What'd you get into last night? Mira and Jaycee?" Roman laughed at his joke, and Cash wanted to punch him in the face.

Nicola grumbled as she stormed out. "You guys are pigs."

Roman nodded toward her. "What's got her all worked up?"

"Maybe you cool it on Mira-Jaycee thing." If Roman noticed that Cash suggested that through clenched teeth, the guy ignored it.

"You know who needs a dose of Mira-Jaycee is Double-deuce."

That was the best idea Cash had heard all day long. Jacob

could have those girls and keep away from Nicola. "At least he wouldn't bother Nic so much."

"Exactly." Roman nodded.

"Or she could always find a guy like me."

"Yeah, not in the mood to go to jail 'cause I'd have to kill any dude like you who touched her."

Cash's molars were going to shatter with all the gnashing going down this morning. "Meaning?"

"Hardy har har, asshole. Like you'd let her go anywhere alone with someone like you. Shit." Roman shook his head, laughing like they shared some funny joke, and Cash could do nothing but ball his hands into fists.

"Right." This was going to be way harder than he thought. Nicola was right. Operation rehab his image needed a serious planning session.

CHAPTER 13

TODAY WAS THE BIG TWO-OH. It was her birthday, and Nicola was at work glaring at her desk. Spreadsheet after spreadsheet. Bank transfers piled high in folders. They weren't that interesting, except for the fact that none of them made sense. Either the account balances were off, or sales totals were wrong because the durable goods and their corresponding accounts were comical. There was an error somewhere, the type where someone accidentally added five zeroes to each dollar amount.

She picked up the phone and dialed her boss. "Hi, Aleena, I'm having the same problem. The numbers look off from the shipping manifest."

Her boss huffed in her ear, again, because this was the second time she'd brought it up.

"No one's paying you to analyze the accounts. Just crunch the numbers and process the bill of sales."

"Even if they're wrong?"

"Ignore the numbers," Aleena snipped and hung up the phone.

This was ridiculous. Nicola was an intern, not a dunce. No

one would buy rolls of fabric at ten thousand dollars a yard. And it wasn't like she was doing books for Prada or Gucci. There was no Louis Vuitton warehouse anywhere in their general vicinity. She was doing the books for a no-name corporation whose warehouse seemed dead except for the occasional flurry, and their profit margins were off. What she thought had been the perfect position was now just a big pain in the butt.

She hung up and continued to analyze the accounts and translate the bills of sale. She swore, if they weren't actually giving her college credit for this internship, the job would amount to nothing but busy work. She checked the time on her screen. Time to go.

Nicola passed three huge guys as she walked out. They were broad, built, and looked scarier than a horror movie. They also looked out of place to be heading into a textile warehouse.

In the parking lot, she slipped into her car, frustrated that the job that she'd jockeyed for was turning to crap fast. "Whatever. It's one semester. You need the credit."

Yeah, talking to herself was a first sign that things weren't going well. As she pulled out of the lot, another dark car with tinted windows arrived. She watched in her rearview mirror, curious to see a buyer of super expensive nothingness, but instead, she saw more huge guys flanking another guy—not as big—but definitely having a worse day than her. That sucked for him, and she channeled her irritation into driving away, slamming on the gas pedal.

Twenty minutes later, she had parked on campus and was walking up the SAC ramp. Her cell buzzed and the screen made her grin. A text from Cash.

How's the bday going?

He'd called her that morning and wished her a very happy, very dirty birthday. It had made her stomach flip, and she hadn't heard from him for the rest of the morning.

Tonight was her birthday party, courtesy of Roman and Cash and the rest of the TKX boys. Something about being Roman's kid sister and Cash's best friend had made her something like campus royalty when she first arrived as a freshman. They'd thrown her the same party last year, but it'd been a surprise. She'd arrived on Cash's arm not expecting a thing. Tonight, one year later, she'd arrive on his arm again. Not a surprise party, but why break the tradition? God, had it really been a year? *How things change.*

She typed out: *Good. Job's driving me crazy.*

The ramp was packed with people heading in and out of the SAC. Everyone had mellowed back into the swing of things, and the usual suspects were hanging out where she'd expect to see them. Football players held court at the top of the ramp. Sorority girls trailed after whichever frat boys their groups fell in line with, and a couple of credit card companies were offering free t-shirts and beer cozies in exchange for sign ups. Her phone buzzed again.

Forget about it. U have super secret date night tonight.

She bit her lip to hide a bigger smile. A second text came through.

I can see you.

Glancing over her shoulder, she stared down the ramp, and her phone buzzed again.

Wrong direction.

Her smile threatened to take over her whole face, a smile

105

that said he made her giddy and giggly. She spun to find him and slammed into Jacob.

Nicola took a step back. "Shit. Sorry."

The ball cap pulled down low looked good on him. Textbook good looking. Add on that he was the popular quarterback with a promising career, and Nic could see why girls swooned. But she could also see that he was confident her ear-to-ear grin had everything to do with running into him. "Look at you smiling like that. What's up?"

"Nothing." But she knew her cheeks were pink, and she looked like she had a secret to hide.

His eyes drifted to her phone. Before she could pull back, he snatched it. "Who you talking to?"

"Not funny, J." What could be classified as harmless flirting had disaster all over it. If he read those texts... *Shit!* She jumped for it. "Give me."

Roaring back with a laugh, he held it high overhead. "Try again!"

She jumped again, panicked. Jacob was about to out her and Cash, all because J thought he was a flirtatious hot stud and she hadn't locked her phone. "Give me my phone."

Jacob spun out of her reach, fake throwing it back to her, spun again like he was auditioning for some ESPN sport reel highlights. *Ugh, asshole!* He faked—no—he *for real* tossed it. The phone arched high over her head. Her fingers reached for it as she turned and slammed into Roman. *What the fuck?*

Roman caught her cell, holding it above her head. "What's going on?"

"Nic's got a secret." J clapped twice, and Roman tossed it back to him.

Seriously, for all the bullshit overprotective crap that Roman said about Jacob, he was going to get all kinds of hell from her for participating in this little game.

"Damn it, Roman. We're not playing monkey in the middle. Give me." She jumped again as Jacob lofted it. "My phone."

"Over here."

Cash. She spun to face him as Roman tossed the phone. He held it up, lazy grin and gorgeous eyes. "You looking for this?"

Her cheeks were on fire. "Yes. My phone. Please."

Cash looked at Roman and Jacob. "Why are we torturing her?" He looked back her way, all knowing. "Not that we need a reason to drive the girl crazy."

In her head, that came out of his mouth loaded with sexual innuendo, probably having something to do with that fact that he drove her crazy, constantly. And even now, with his hand holding her phone high, his chest was broad and cut, while the muscles in his arm were chiseled to tan perfection.

Jacob motioned for Cash to toss the phone, and if he did that, he was a dead man. A hot sex-god of a dead man because she'd kill him.

"She's all smiles and giggles over something." J acted like he was cute. "Seems like we should know, given that she never smiles and giggles."

"Ah, Nicola has a secret boyfriend." Cash teased. "Let's see."

"Give me my phone, Cash."

He scrolled through her cell and bunched his forehead, mock-studying her screen. "She loves… Wait for it…

107

Accounting." He shook his head. "Sorry to get your hopes up, Double-deuce—"

Jacob scowled at Cash. "No one said anything about hopes up, dude. Just giving the girl hell."

Roman nodded. "No one's getting any hope up about Nic. Shit. Not now. Not ever. Certainly not you."

"I'm still here, you know." She snagged her phone from Cash, and he let his fingers drift over her skin. *Oh...* He did that on purpose, and it was insanely awesome. A cascading rush of shivers ran up her arm. "I can see whoever I want. Thank you very much."

"I didn't say I was trying to see you." Jacob's bruised ego was on PR duty. "And I'm not as bad as Cash."

Roman chuckled. "No shit."

Now it was her turn to furrow brows. "No one asked you."

Cash crossed his arms over his chest and didn't join in the banter. She wasn't sure if that was a good thing—because he looked to be one snide comment away from kissing her to stake a claim.

She locked her phone and took off up the ramp. J said something about going to class, Roman said something about ditching class, and Cash said nothing but fell in step with her.

"Hey," he said.

"That was close."

He shook his head. "It was fine. Don't sweat it."

"I'm serious, Cash. That was almost awful."

"You need a distraction."

"Maybe." Really, she needed to hang out with guys who didn't find entertainment in torturing her.

"Don't forget about super-secret date night, birthday girl."

He threw his arm around her shoulders. "Come on. We'll grab some lunch, and I'll walk you to class. The entire time you can think about…" He leaned over and whispered, "Exactly how I'll make you come tonight."

All over again, hot cheeks and stolen breath. God, she loved him.

CHAPTER 14

CLASSES WERE DONE FOR THE day, and Cash was ready for tonight. He shut the front door behind him and saw Roman kicked back on the couch, tossing a football in the air.

"Heads up."

"Hey." The ball sailed over, and Cash snagged it. Heading to the fridge for a beer, he tossed it back at the couch.

"You ready for tonight?" Roman went back to tossing the ball in the air.

Twisting the cap off the bottle, he took a long pull before facing the couch. "Yeah, should be fun."

"You think something's up with Birthday Girl?"

After another long pull, Cash shrugged. "What do you mean?"

Roman tossed the ball at him. "She seems preoccupied."

Sounded about right. That was how he felt too, and she was the root cause, but that wasn't a conversation he needed to dig into now. Better to redirect. "I think she hates her job."

"Maybe." Ball toss. "But that's not it. I haven't seen her much lately. Hell, you either."

Cash choked on his beer. "She's doing her own thing. That's cool, I guess."

Roman scowled. "Long as it's not with Jacob."

"No shit." Cash stared at the long neck, feeling like a piece of shit for keeping Roman in the dark. "If she wanted to though, you probably need to give her a break."

"Good thing she's not stupid."

Agreed, but jumping on the Jacob-hating bandwagon wouldn't do any good. "Here's the thing about Nicola."

Roman's brows rose. "You're going to tell me something I don't know about my own sister?"

Cash shrugged. "Maybe."

"Right."

"She's smart. Sweet. Popular. Like it or not, the girl's hot." Roman pegged the ball at him. Cash caught it and laughed, shaking his head. "See, dude?"

"And all that has nothing to do with her being distracted."

"She's not a kid anymore, and, really, hasn't been for a while. So maybe she's distracted. Or maybe she's just scared to talk to you about whatever."

Roman jumped up, headed to the kitchen, and grabbed a beer. He cracked the top and drained half of it before turning back to Cash. "I'm glad you're bringing her over to the house tonight. If she showed up with Brandy or Hannah or whoever, she'd look like fair game."

And Cash would have to kill someone. Then everyone would know whether Nicola liked it or not. "Well, then I guess we just have to pretend she's with me."

Roman threw his head back. "The devil we know."

———————————

"YOU'RE NOT MY SUPER-SECRET birthday date if everyone sees your hands all over me." Nic walked like a robot. Her arms and legs moved choppily, and Cash would've laughed if she hadn't been so nervous. Every few seconds, she tugged on her shirt, checked her cell phone, or pushed his hands off of her.

He loved it. "That's what's fun about this."

"What? Having to ignore you on my birthday?"

"Loosen up. Just like last year, nobody will think twice that you're here with me."

"Last year, you weren't touching me like you are now."

"Don't think I didn't want to, sweet girl."

They stood near the side door to the TKX house. Base bumped through the windows. A couple of folks were outside smoking cigarettes, but everyone else was inside. "Think of it like foreplay."

Her jaw dropped, eyes bugged, and she looked around like he'd said it with a megaphone. "Oh my God, Cash."

Foreplay it was, because her acting all innocent and untouchable was about to drive him clean off the edge.

"Happy birthday," came from a few folks.

She waved and giggled. A couple wandering sets of eyes drifted over her, poking his possessive-alpha tendencies, and he was losing his cool before they'd even walked inside.

"Cash?"

His chest felt tight. "Yeah, babe."

"Your turn to calm down. Take a breath already."

That transparent, huh? Maybe just to her. They were getting good at reading each other. "Trying." He realized that this may be harder than he'd thought. As long as he kept his hands on her, he'd be fine.

"Hey." Even in high heels, she had to go up on tiptoes to reach his cheek. She pecked him quickly. Flirty, friendly, nothing that would raise too many eyebrows. "Think of it like foreplay."

Her cheeks blushed as she said the word. It took about everything he had not to celebrate her birthday someplace else far, far away, and totally naked.

The side door flew open, and a few girls he knew squeaked and squawked, drunk and eyeing him like they all wanted his attention. He took a step forward, passing them, and grabbed the door. "Here we go."

He pushed up behind Nic, letting the crowd of bodies hide his hands roaming on her waist, and whispered, "Alrighty, let's have some fun, so I can take you home."

There were people everywhere, and he needed to get her some fruity chick drink and him a beer, or they'd never relax. With Nicola in front of him, he leaned over, arms draping over her shoulders. "Move it, people. Birthday girl coming through."

Finally at the bar, he grabbed a beer and shouted for something pink. A nod from one of the pledges on bartending duty, and that something pink with a straw arrived. She looked pleased enough and took three long pulls.

He sipped his beer, surveying the room. Everywhere he

looked, people waved hey. Some offered Nic birthday shots. Wasn't really her thing to down as many shots as her age, but if that was what she wanted, he wasn't going to tell her no. But she smiled, scrunching her nose, waving away some offers, downing others.

"Better now?" he asked.

"Getting there." She leaned against him, and his hands had her hips. "You?"

"Getting there." The place smelled like stale beer and too many bodies, but with her this close, he could smell her shampoo. The swell of her ass swayed against him. "Where you want to go? Upstairs? Out on the deck?"

Nicola sighed. "Think anyone would notice if we left?"

"Are you trying to take me home already?"

She wiggled her eyebrows. "Absolutely."

"You haven't seen your roomies or Roman."

"I can see them anytime."

He leaned over, letting his lips tickle the top of her ear. "But you can have me anytime too."

She turned in his arms, and nothing about the way they were pinned together looked like friends. He took her drink and set it at the bar. His heart beat into his throat, and his mind raced. His hand snaked around her waist and pulled her closer. Just to taste her lips. Just to hear her sigh. To say his name like she'd done before. Breathy and wanting.

"Cash…"

Just like that. "Yeah?"

There was no space between them, and he didn't care. The base thumped around them, and the lights were low. Too many people were too close, but the crowd was their camouflage. No one could see how they clung together. No one noticed how her eyes locked to him. Or if they did, he didn't notice them.

Cash backed them toward the center of the living room, a makeshift dance floor filled with people dancing, talking, drinking. But it was only them. The brash and the booze, it drifted away as her fingers crawled up his chest and locked behind his neck.

She went on tiptoes, he thought to say something. Acting like it was a secret that she had to whisper, he leaned to her, still holding her close, the curve of her breasts firmly against him. But her tongue teased his ear. Hot breath tortured him. A sly kiss hidden by her arms wrapped around his head, holding them in place. Swaying to music—

"Nicola!" A drunk Double-deuce came out of nowhere. "Excuse me, Cash." He tried to step between them. "Wanna dance, babe?"

No way in hell. Primal possessiveness gripped Cash's chest. "Back off, Jacob."

Jacob threw his head back, laughing like he didn't know he was about to have his face pummeled to a pulp. "Cash, man." His eyes trailed over Nicola. "Goddamn, Nicola."

Hell no. Dude was going to have serious problems if he looked at his girl that way again. Drunk hands reached for her.

"Not in the mood, J." She smacked the reaching hand. Smart girl. Definitely less problematic for her to slap him away than for Cash to break his wrist.

"Nicky."

She smirked. "Don't call me that."

"Get out of here, Jacob." The words rumbled out of Cash's chest as his hands clasped around her waist.

Cash spun them away, grinding his teeth together. One step away, and Jacob clapped a hand on Cash's shoulder. His jaw flexed, and a whole lot of *the fuck he did* coursed through his brain.

"Get your motherfuckin' hand off me." Cash turned, seeing red, but also saw Roman out of the corner of his eye. Cash shook off Jacob. "Nic, head toward your brother."

"What? Wait. No." She tried to turn back, but the crowd jostled around them.

A staggering Jacob reached for Nicola, but Cash stepped in front of him. "Back off, Jacob."

Nicola jumped between him and Jacob. "Don't do this, Cash. Don't."

Jacob swayed on his feet, pawing at her. She batted him off, but he leaned for her again. "Nic wants to dance. Dontcha?"

The music pumped loud as the beat in Cash's heart. Blood rushed in his ears, and tunnel vision was fast approaching. She needed to go. Jacob needed to back the hell off. "I swear to God, Nicola, go find Roman—"

Roman arrived, hooked an arm around her, tugging her back. "Let's go."

"Damn it, all of you," Nicola yelled.

Jacob squared off against Cash. "What's your problem?"

A few football players lined up behind Jacob. They looked more curious about the happenings than ready to throw down. But even if they did, Cash was sure his anger and agility would topple Jacob. Hell, the way he was feeling, bring on the entire team. A couple of TKXs buzzed behind his back. Nicola was a few feet away, giving Roman ten shades of hell and cursing both Cash and Jacob.

Jacob swayed, stepping forward, leering and looking for a fight. "What is it with you and that girl? She ain't yours, country boy."

Wrong. Cash let his fist fly. Jacob's head snapped back. All that brawn didn't do shit when he was tanked. He staggered back, shook his head, then charged.

Jacob might've been built as broad as a dorm, but his reach didn't do much. The few blows that landed were unnoticeable. Cash was tall and fast. He hooked right then left. Not a soul jumped in. No one pulled him back. The music died, but the crowd roared. Didn't matter, all he saw was Jacob leering at her, and it wouldn't happen again.

"Stop!" Nicola screamed.

At that moment, he would've stood on top of the bar, pointed to her, claimed her as his, and been done with it.

Balled fists hanging down, he looked at the football players. They watched their boy but didn't make a move. A trickle of blood ran out Jacob's nose, but his hands went up.

"What the fuck, Cash?" Still swaying, Jacob bowed out, shook off the rah-rah from his boys, and headed toward the front door.

Damn it, the guy was his boy. Kind of. Hell. It didn't matter. Cash shook out his fist, felt the adrenaline still coursing through his blood. He shouldered back through the crowd. Roman's jaw was tight, and he gave him a nod, a thank you for knocking the shit out of someone who had said the wrong thing to his sister. But then Cash saw Nicola. Tears streamed down her face. His stomach bottomed out, and he hurt more than any punch Double-deuce had landed. *Fuck.*

The music blasted again. The scrap was a short-winded blip in the night, forgotten already as girls gossiped, dancing started, and drinks were poured.

"Nic," he shouted toward her, but she spun away under the mass of hugs from a group of girls. Roman stepped around them as the girls disappeared into the crowd. TKXs surrounded them. Roman was talking to him. Too close to a speaker, Cash couldn't even hear himself. "Nicola!"

Roman was in his face. "Dude. She's fine. Brandy's got her."

Cash pushed past him. Sweat poured down his back. "Nic."

God, had he lost his freakin' mind? Maybe. He was going to tear the walls down if he couldn't get to her. Had he seriously made her cry? On her damn birthday? *Fuck. Fuck, man. Just fuck. Fucking Jacob. Fucking secrets.*

By the pool tables, he caught sight of Brandy and Nicola walking toward the front hall. He pushed through the crowd and watched them duck into the ladies room. He used a balled up fist to knock twice. "Coming in."

"Shit, Cash. Get out of here." Brandy had her arms crossed, and Nicola wouldn't look at him. "Go."

"Go away, Brandy."

"No. Ladies room. Not a tough concept. Out."

"Brandy—"

"Out!"

"Nic—"

She spun. "No. You don't get to act like that."

Act like what? Shit. "He's drunk."

"He's our friend."

"He crossed the line."

"Says you."

"Watch yourself, sweet girl."

Nicola scowled at him. "Tonight sucks."

Well, damn that hurt. Super-secret date night on her birthday wasn't supposed to go like this, but hell, when no one knew she was with him, of course she was going to get hit on.

Brandy told the two other girls in the bathroom to leave. Nicola turned from him and rubbed the makeup smudges under her eyes.

"Cash," Brandy said. "Whatever you want with that girl, you can't go around punching people because they look at her."

"He did more than look."

"But not a whole lot more. You and Roman need to back off. Or you need to do something about it. Either—"

"Leave him alone, Brandy." Nicola had her hands propped on the counter, but her head was down, shoulders sagging. "Just give me a minute to talk to him."

Brandy glared at him then smiled at her. "I'll be out here if you need anything."

"She doesn't need anything." He opened the door, ushering her out.

After it closed, he leaned against it. "What do you want from me, Nic? I can't say anything. I can't do anything. I've agreed to keep quiet. But, shit, dude comes near you again..." He shook his head, dropping it back to stare at the ceiling like an answer to his frustration was painted up there. Nope. He brought his gaze back to her.

Once they'd owned up to dating, he'd all but have her name tattooed across his chest. *Taken by Nicola Hart.* She was the type of girl that forever and then some was made for, but what was the point of dating someone if forever wasn't anticipated? Maybe that's why he'd never dated before. Forever had never been an option.

But with Nicola it was.

Not even an option. Or anticipation. It was a fact.

Holy what-the-fucks.

He was going to marry her one day. And why shouldn't he?

Everything he'd ever wanted in a girl was all teary-eyed and aggravated but still standing in front of him. There was no place in the world he rather be than trying to convince her to walk out of that bathroom and hold up a *he's with me* sign.

His heart pounded. Cash scrubbed his hands over his face and ran them into his hair. This semester and the next left, then he'd be done with school. She still had two more years. But—

"Cash?"

He looked at her, never more confident than he was at that second. "Yeah?"

She tilted her head. "What's that look?"

"That's the look of a guy going home with his girl." He walked over, hooked his arms around her, and dragged his lips over hers. "Despite super-secret date night fail on your birthday."

She grinned. "Maybe."

120

"I'm new at this dating thing. Give me a break."

A loud knock hit the bathroom door. "Nicola?"

Roman. Cash took a step back.

"Cash in there with you?"

"Yeah. I am." He pulled the door, and Roman walked in.

"What the shit happened out there?"

Nicola went back to rubbing off smudged make up. "J got out of line. Cash told him to stop. He didn't listen, and if it wasn't Cash, it would've been you."

Roman still looked concerned. "Jacob's an ass. But you're okay?"

"I'm fine. A little sick of you two always acting like you have to protect my honor or something. The guy just wanted to dance."

Roman shook his head. "That guy wants way more that—"

"If I wanted him to, you couldn't stop him from dating me."

Whoa there. "Point made, Nic. I'd stop that conversation before it goes anywhere." Because Cash wasn't going to put up with hypotheticals about her doing anything with Jacob just so she could torque her brother.

Roman crossed his arms over his chest. "Nicola, there's a difference between hanging with Double-deuce and you *hanging* with the guy. You don't need that."

"I'm not sure I've ever come across a guy you do think I should *hang* with." She used air quotes.

"You're right." Roman looked about as comfortable with the topic as Cash felt. "Not a single guy out there is worth your time. That's why you have us: to keep the scum away."

121

This conversation wasn't going anywhere helpful.

"I need to get out of here." She balled up a towel and tossed it. "Cash, take me home. I'm done."

Roman turned his head. "You mind?"

Hell no. "I'll survive."

"Thanks, man." He clapped Cash on the back and opened the door. "Gotta keep the pieces of shit away from our girl."

CHAPTER 15

THE COOL NIGHT AIR WHISKED over her as she pushed out the back door of the TKX house. Cash was behind her and hadn't said a word since she'd said goodnight to Brandy and Hannah. Both gave him dirty looks. She couldn't blame them, correct them, gossip, or gush to them. It wasn't the greatest situation.

At the far end of the parking lot, standing at his truck's door, she waited impatiently for him to click it open. But he didn't. Instead, he walked up behind her, pressing her against the cold metal door.

"What should we do to save super-secret date night? It's still your birthday for another hour or so. Whatever you want." He closed the space between them. His stomach touched her back. Everything about him was deliciously muscled. Looming behind her, he held her against the door, and her heart beat faster. Anyone could walk by. Anyone could see them.

"I think it's a lost cause."

Slowly, his lazy smile danced in his voice. "Nah. We just need another date idea."

Shivers slid down her neck. She whispered, "It's late."

He leaned closer to her ear. "So?"

"So…" Her heart pounded faster. Louder. They were so obvious, but she couldn't break from the warmth radiating between them. "Date nights are dinners and movies. We're past a normal date night."

"We're not normal anything, and you're all dressed up for your special day." His words tickled her ear. He brushed the hair off her neck, dragging his fingers across her skin. "Lookin' hotter than sin. I might be new at this dating thing, but it can't be that hard to come up with something, because I'm not ready to take you home and tear off your clothes quite yet."

Her lungs clenched. She wanted to breathe—maybe—but couldn't, not when his body rubbed against her, promising what she dreamed of.

"A date." She gasped when he leaned his weight against her. "Like…"

Like what? She couldn't think of anything except what he'd just said. His promise to take her clothes off was the only thing she could focus on.

"Like…" His hand smoothed down her back, settling on the back of her skirt. "Well." He turned her around. "Maybe we don't need a date. Maybe I make good use of this skirt and a dark parking lot."

Her jaw dropped. "You can't be serious."

"You think I'm not?" His palms rubbed her waist, sliding down the top of her thighs, smoothing back up and tugging the skirt only to let it go before it became indecent.

"Someone will see us."

He nipped at her ear. "Probably not."

She could barely catch her breath. It was dark. The truck wasn't near a street lamp. "Probably." That sounded as breathy and wispy as she felt. "There's a definite chance."

His fingers slid down the skirt again, and this time, they drifted onto her skin, sliding and smoothing as he bent closer and kissed her neck. Her mind scrambled. He pinned her against the truck, his erection swollen behind his jeans. She rolled her head to the side, giving him all the access he wanted to her neck, and his mouth was insane heaven, more than she could comprehend, hot and wicked and making everything inside her body cry for his attention.

"This is so wrong," she moaned.

His teeth bit down. Her hands reached for his jeans, finding the button, the zipper, and he reached for his pocket. Condom on in seconds, he lifted her up and pushed her thong to the side.

"So wrong," he agreed as he pressed against her.

Panting and clinging to him, she was more than ready as he thrust into her. Her breath stopped, eyes rolled, and jaw slowly dropped. Unreal how good he felt.

His eyes locked onto hers. "You okay?"

Butterflies spun from her stomach to her lungs. She nodded, and he pumped deeper. Her eyes slammed shut at the intensity, the complete, incredible, all-encompassing fulfillment.

This was dangerous. Everything she'd just begged for, secrets and hiding, and here she was, having sex with Cash against his truck. In a parking lot where hundreds of people were close enough to hear if she lost control and screamed his name. And hell, the things he was doing to her, the way he owned her body.

God, she could hear herself moaning, feel the cold metal against her back. Their clothes still on and rubbing her nipples. His skin rubbed against her clit. She drew her legs up, wrapped her arms around his neck, and a wild climax built deep inside, threatening to echo across campus.

Nicola bit against his shoulder, his shirt-covered flesh catching her teeth and tongue. Rippling tides of orgasm rushed through her. She would cave in on herself if it was possible, falling apart as he pounded into her.

The sounds of him coming with her burned into her memory. They were panting, gasping, interlocked, and unmoving.

Hands threading into her hair, he breathed against her ear. "Holy hell."

Holy hell was right. That was insane.

Carefully letting her down, he stepped away, and she checked that her skirt was down. He made fast work of taking care of business. Then they stood there. She couldn't move. Her legs were boneless. And he…he had a look in his eye that she couldn't define.

Reaching around her, Cash opened the door to his truck and lifted her inside. "One of these days, we should have sex inside. Maybe even with a bed. Not that I'm complaining."

Her cheeks went hot, but he saved her from responding when he closed the door, looking somehow sweeter and cockier than ever.

A second later, he was walking around the front of the truck, talking on his cell phone. He stayed outside, leaning against the door, and she couldn't hear the conversation.

Finally, he turned, opened the door, and grinned. "I'm a genius. Super-secret date night is back on, birthday girl."

CHAPTER 16

SUPER-SECRET DATE NIGHT WAS back on? Cash must've been crazy. It was late, and nothing was open. "What are we doing?"

"Something awesome." He turned the truck's engine over and revved it.

"And that is?"

Cash gave her a look that made her melt, then he pulled out of his parking spot, driving toward the backside of campus. "Someplace awesome."

"Something and someplace *awesome*. Got it. So?"

"So, nothing. You'll have fun."

"You're not going to tell me?"

No answer. But he didn't stop smiling. Instead, he pulled her under his arm, driving with just a wrist thrown over the steering wheel. Two minutes later, they pulled into the parking lot at the science complex.

She looked around. Everything was dark. "What are we—"

"Stop with all the questions, and come on."

He'd never led her astray before, and whatever they were

doing, he was pumped. She hopped out and let him pull her toward the building. They passed the front doors. Orange plastic fencing marked off the new wing under construction, and he pulled up the plastic and ducked under. Still holding it high enough that she didn't have to crawl, he tilted his head. "This way, birthday girl."

This way to be arrested? A HARD HAT ZONE sign loomed. "Where are we—"

"Shh," he hushed her like he was getting ready to hide, making her stomach free fall to her knees. Then he laughed. "Kidding."

"Cash!" She elbowed him, making him laugh harder. "Breaking and entering isn't a good date idea. I know you know that."

"We're not." They rounded the corner. "We've got the keys. Kinda." A guy a little older than them leaned against a set of doors. "Hey, man. Thanks."

"You owe me, Cash." The guy nodded to her. "Hi, I'm Gary."

Unsure of this addition to their twosome, she smiled hesitantly. "Hi."

Cash interlaced his fingers with hers. "This is Nicola. She's a secret. You never saw us together."

She swatted his chest. "You're horrible. But, hi, um, thanks." Thanks for what? She had no idea, and hopefully she wasn't thanking a guy she'd be in the back of a cop car with.

"No problem." Gary shifted, fumbling in his pockets. "Just happy to be a part of history."

"History?" She looked at Cash.

He shook his head with a half a grin on his handsome

face. "Don't be an asshole, or I forget about that favor I owe you."

Gary nodded. "Just playing. But seriously, it's good to meet the girl who makes this guy go straight and narrow." He turned toward the door and unlocked it.

"Um…" She went on tiptoes in her heels. "Should we be doing this?"

Cash shook his head. "Nope."

"Oh." Well, at least he was honest.

Construction tarps lined the ground, and she racked her brain about something she'd read last spring in the school paper. The school was expanding. There was constant construction. But this made the news over a touristy-educational thing. Maybe a museum. She couldn't remember, but it wasn't campus lecture halls and lab rooms.

Gary went ahead of them and flipped a few lights, and Cash followed. "The place is coming along quickly, should be done any day now. Anyway, the doors will lock behind you when you're done. Walk through there, and you'll be set."

Even with the few lights turned on, it was still really dark. Almost chilly. But it was the air of not-supposed-to-be-here that made her shiver. Cash rubbed his thumb over her knuckles. "Ready for awesome?"

They passed through a door, and then—

Wow.

A sleek glass tunnel surrounded them with water on all sides, as though they were in a fish tank. Dark blue and purple lights lit the water. Giant, brightly colored fish swam above them. Tiny neon fish shot past, changing direction en mass among rocks, sand, and swaying plants. She had no words.

"What do you think?" He walked them down the tunnel. "It'd be cooler if there was music or something."

A giant creature floated above them. "I can't believe this is here."

They weren't super close to the coastline, but the ocean wasn't that far away either. And it being a terrific school, grant writing and academics and all that, there were always new things arriving on campus. But this…this was unreal.

The aquarium wasn't huge, probably just large enough so the science department could study and research and the school could make money on tourists…but this was crazy.

"Told you it'd be awesome."

Yeah, he had. "It's like a hidden world." The tunneled hall dead-ended in an ocean of swaying lights.

"Very cool, right? I play poker with Gary. He works construction here and told me about these bad boys over the summer. No one really knows they're here yet."

"Why did he let us in? He could lose his job, right?"

Cash walked her in front of him, his arms wrapping under hers and locking around her stomach. "We're buddies."

"That's not a *why*. He just let—"

"I told him I had to figure out this dating thing on the quick, and it was your birthday. Tonight could've gone better, and I don't like to fail. And shit, sweet girl, other than you, this was the prettiest thing I could think of. Seemed like I might redeem myself."

Her jaw dropped. "No way you told him all that."

He laughed, turning them toward a giant fish that floated by. "Sounded good though, right?"

"This is pretty romantic, Cash."

He shifted. "I know zip about romance."

"What do you know?"

"What do I know…?" He hummed. "I know I'm glad I'm with you. There aren't any redos in life. There's nothing that will bring me to this moment again. It's your birthday. It's a Friday. I don't know, why even pretend to need an excuse? All I need is you."

She shook her head, and he loosened his grip around her to brush some hair back behind her ears.

"Does that make sense?"

She blinked. "I…"

He laughed. "Glad we cleared that up."

Minutes ticked by. "You like me that much?"

"Not even going to answer that."

Sighing, she leaned against his chest. "You've redeemed yourself on super-secret date night."

They walked through the tunnel until it ended in the igloo of lights. Hundreds, maybe thousands of fish as bright as nature might allow swam in every direction.

He kissed her. Nicola ran her hands up his neck and into his hair, fingers threading, tugging. She liked how confident she was becoming in his arms.

Two long strides of him half-carrying, half-kissing her, he had her on a bench, letting his lips linger. "All I had to do was say *I want you* after a B & E. No idea how I'm going to top this one."

She laughed.

"So what do you think?" he asked.

She toyed with the sleeve of his t-shirt. "Unreal. Just…perfect."

"Not about me, sweet girl. The fish."

She laughed again and burrowed close. "You're awful."

"You like me," he said.

"I do."

Cash's eyes narrowed, and he cleared his throat. "Happy birthday. May all your dreams come true."

CHAPTER 17

NICOLA WOKE UP TO BRANDY and Hannah staring down at her. Their looks said there was gossip to be shared. But as Nicola rubbed her eyes, she realized *she* was the gossip. Fun…

"Wake up, and spit it out. Now." Brandy's hands were on her hips. "Start talking."

Still rubbing the sleep out of her eyes, Nicola knew exactly what Brandy was talking about and decided the best course of action was to play stupid. "Nothing to talk about."

Hannah smiled. "I saw Cash dropping you off last night."

Great. Thanks, Hannah. How long had she stayed in his truck kissing him good night? "So you told Brandy what? You saw Cash dropping me off? Big deal." She pulled the blankets over her head. "Go away."

"You're going to explain what happened with Jacob then? Or what the hell happened between you and Cash in the bathroom?" Brandy asked.

Both girls dropped onto the bed. Hannah patted her blanket-covered head. "Seriously, if something is going on there, you *have* to tell us. Come out and fess up."

Nicola pulled the covers down a little bit. "Say I have a thing for him."

Brandy rolled her eyes. "Then I'd say, no shit."

"I'm being serious. Say I did. And I thought he did too. Then…"

Hannah asked, "Then what?"

Brandy beamed. "Then you tell us every single stinkin' detail. That's what."

"No. I mean. You think Roman's going to flip out?"

Brandy cackled. "Well, yeah. He's halfway to psycho on regular Joes. You doing his best friend? Guy's going to go off the deep end. It's Cash, no less."

Nic pulled the cover back over her head. "No one's doing anyone." That was a lie. A big one.

Brandy pulled it back down. "You haven't slept with him?"

Nic's stomach flipped, and her perma-smile reappeared. "No way."

"Oh my God." Brandy covered her wide open mouth. "You—"

"No freakin' way." Hannah nudged Brandy. "Right, Nic? I mean… Right? You would've told us."

"Right." Lying to her best friends was so wrong. "I can't get him out of my head."

Hannah squealed. "Have you kissed him?"

Nic shrugged. "Maybe."

"Holy shit." Brandy smacked the bed. "Roman's going to kill Cash. Bang, bang, he's dead."

"Maybe not…" She cringed.

"Cash is totally a player, Nic. You know that."

"Brandy's right, *but...*" Hannah sliced Brandy a look. "Since you guys are friends and all, it won't be like that. Right?"

Brandy smirked right back. "You don't seriously think Cash will—"

Hannah smacked her leg. "Brandy!"

Nicola pulled the covers back up. "He wouldn't hurt me."

"So what are you going to do about it? You can't let him walk around starting fights with guys when no one knows you two are...whatever you two are."

"We're nothing."

"I don't believe that." Brandy shook her head. "Cash is all... And you're all—"

"I kissed him!" Saying it out loud felt awesome.

"Shut up!" Brandy bounced. "Just, holy freakin' shit."

"I knew it." Hannah squealed again. "And... Come on, girl! Details?"

"In the pool."

Brandy's jaw dropped. "You had sex with him in our pool?"

"No! Oh my God. I said *kissed.*"

"You also said *Cash,* so I figured—"

"He's not like that."

Brandy rolled her eyes. "He's *so* like that."

"Maybe not with her, bitch."

"Thank you, Hannah."

Another eye roll from Brandy. "So you haven't slept with him?"

Nicola bit her lip.

"Holy fucking shit." Brandy smacked the bed with each word. "I can*not* believe you didn't tell us."

"I haven't told anyone. Not until we tell Roman. Not that I'd say I was sleeping with Cash. Dating might be a better word. Ugh, I don't know."

"So this is like a thing. Like a real…thing?" Hannah asked.

"I think so." Nic's cheeks flamed, and she pulled the covers tighter. "I'm afraid if I say it out loud, I'll jinx it. Like it'll just, poof, disappear. I don't want him going anywhere."

"I just can't believe it." Brandy drew out the words. "Spit out the details. Now."

"*No way.*" Nicola shook her head.

"Summary description then," Brandy countered. The girl would make a good lawyer or something one day. She could badger her way to the truth.

Nicola pinched her eyes, then peeled the covers down and gave a two-minute recap from faking her stomachache to his thumb smoothing over her knuckles, her cheek, her chin, then the dinner that turned into a camp out, and sex under the stars, *and* up against the truck, then sneaking into the aquarium, and the nickname that he'd started using for her. She felt herself smiling through the whole story. She looked up, rolling her bottom lip into her mouth. "So…"

Both Hannah and Brandy sat perfectly still on her bed. Perfectly quiet. Their mouths hung perfectly open.

"You guys, say something." Her nerves would get the best of her if they didn't say something. Anything.

Brandy shut her mouth, then Hannah closed hers. Brandy spoke first. "I got nothing."

"Sweet girl?" Hannah asked.

She nodded. "Cute, right?"

"Uh, yeah."

"Brandy? You, silent, is kinda freaking me out."

"Like I said, I got nothing." Brandy sighed. "I think I may've just fallen in love with Cash Garrison for you even though I don't trust him. At all."

No need to volunteer for that. Nic was far past love. "You don't have to. I'm already there."

TONIGHT NICOLA'S FOLKS WERE THROWING her a birthday cookout. Hannah and Brandy had piled into her car, and the hour drive to her hometown passed quickly. Her mind raced, and she tried to answer all of Brandy and Hannah's questions, but really, she didn't say much. The time on the road let them gush and gossip, and that was good enough, even without every scandalous detail.

She pulled into the driveway and sighed at her safe haven. Everything had remained the same over the years, and it was comforting. The door was partially open, meaning Roman and Cash were already there. Somewhere. Playing ball with her dad maybe? Doing whatever they usually did.

Mom stepped out, phone pressed to her ear, waving hello. Brandy and Hannah hopped out of her car, making their way inside. She took her time. Her mom could read her, and after an hour plus of talking about Cash non-stop, she needed to put her game face on. Telling Roman was one thing, but telling Mom? Mom would tell Dad, and not that Dad overreacted to the male species like Roman did, but he did know that Cash was a bit wild. And as far as she was concerned, she didn't want her dad thinking about her dating anyone, much less the unattainable bachelor that everyone thought they knew so well.

Nicola wandered inside, threw her purse by the couch, and made her way into the kitchen. Mom still chatted on the phone to someone, and her roomies were outside with Roman, Cash, and Dad. She would absolutely, positively kill Brandy if she accidentally let slip any Cash-Nic-hookup details.

Hearing the click of the cordless phone onto the receiver, she turned around. "Hey. Was that Cash's mom?"

"Yes."

"Are they coming over for dinner?"

"Not today. We're going outlet shopping this week."

"Fun." Nicola rummaged through the fruit bowl. Her mom and Cash's mom had always been close. Maybe that was how their three musketeers routine had started. She wondered what his mom would think of her with Cash. "Fun."

"You just said that."

Nicola blinked. "Oh, sorry."

She opened the fridge, grabbed a half gallon of OJ and two glasses. "Something on your mind?"

"Work stuff."

"Work has you stargazing into a bowl of apples?"

Nicola shrugged. "I met a guy."

Mom smiled sweetly. "A guy, huh? Anyone I know?"

"There are like a thousand guys at school."

Now was Mom's turn to shrug. "You never know. Small world. So?"

"So…not much to say about him, I guess." She probably expected more because that'd been Nic's track record. They'd shared everything. Well, Nicola had shared just about everything except for anything having to do with Cash. "But anyway, I think he likes me."

Another sweet, all-knowing, motherly smile. "Of course he does."

Nicola needed to change subjects. "But really, that's not my problem."

"Then what is?"

"My boss is awful. My job sucks big time. And I swear to God, they aren't what they seem."

"Jobs stink in general, angel."

"It more than stinks to high heaven. It's like something's up."

"Sharpening your PI skills, are you?"

"I'm serious, Mom. They're sketch."

She crossed her arms. "Why?"

"Because their numbers and their products don't make sense."

"How long have you worked there now?"

Nicola shrugged. "Couple of weeks."

"So learn what you can, and move on." She walked to the sink and washed vegetables.

"That's a very motherly thing to say."

Mom laughed. "What do you want me to say? Hack into their mainframe? Sneak into their offices? Search high and low for damning evidence?"

That might have been her sort-of-already-started plan. "Maybe."

Still laughing, she shook her head. "I'm sure it's nothing. Do your job. Get your credit. Be done with it, and chalk it up to a learning experience."

Nicola took a long drink of her juice. "Whatever."

"Go tell your dad that he needs to stop playing ball and to flip those steaks. That grill's starting to smoke."

"'Kay."

"And have Cash come talk to me."

Nic's jaw gaped for a moment. "Why?"

"His mom's surprise party is coming up." She tilted her head slightly. "Was there something else I needed to chat with him about?"

Nicola's eyebrows were arched, and her eyes were wide, both reactions that she needed to tone down ASAP. "Nope. Just wondering."

The unforgettable sound of Mom's laughter followed her out the door. Awesome.

THE WEATHER WAS COOL ENOUGH that they didn't eat outside. Everyone piled into the dining room. Roman carried the steaks, Cash grabbed a huge platter of corn, and Dad gave Nicola a big hug just because.

Hannah and Brandy walked in with her mom, and everyone started a game of musical chairs. Hannah sat first. Cash sat down. Roman sat down. Brandy scowled. Hannah popped up, sitting next to Brandy. Both of them giggled like they were in third grade and made a big show that Nicola

CRISTIN HARBER

should sit next to Cash. Cash figured out what was going on and leaned back in his chair, amused. Roman had no idea and asked Brandy why she was making so much noise.

Finally, everyone was seated. Food was served. The guys drank their beers. Nicola's mom brought in a pitcher of lemonade.

"How's the semester going?" Dad offered up to any takers.

A clatter of comments and complaints about school rushed, but Nicola sat back.

"You're awfully quiet, Nicky." Her dad knew her too well. "How was your birthday?"

Brandy coughed on her corn. Nicola glared at her, regretting her decision to share the sex-against-the-truck story. "Fine."

"Fine?" Cash laughed. "She was the belle of the ball."

Roman shook his head. "TKX threw her a party. Other than Jacob, it was a good time."

"Jacob?" Mom looked at her.

She shook her head. "Football player friend."

Dad smiled. "Isn't the quarterback named Jacob? Same guy?"

"Yup." She took a bite of steak.

Cash's brows furrowed. So did Roman's.

Mom smiled. "Is that who—"

"No, Mom." Would this meal ever end?

"Is that who, what?" Cash leaned forward.

Roman shook his head. "Jacob's a dick."

"Mouth," Mom said. "Save it for the backyard, not my dinner table."

142

"Yes, ma'am." Then her brother shoveled in more steak, turning to Dad to talk sports.

Cash smiled at her, and Nicola felt like the entire room could read her mind and knew what had been happening. Brandy laughed, and Hannah hushed her. So maybe at least two people had mind-reading abilities. But they didn't know the half of it. No way could anyone feel as far gone for a guy as she was over Cash.

"Star gazing still?" her mom whispered as she walked by with an empty lemonade pitcher in hand.

Busted.

Brandy and Hannah dissolved into a gossipy, giggly fit. Nic would kill them later. Roman and Dad were in a hot debate about something that'd been on the news, and Cash winked at her before joining in their discussion.

When her mom came back to the table offering lemonade refills, Nicola knew she knew. She had to, and Mom would tell Dad. Maybe. She was a daddy's girl. So maybe mom would keep it to herself and let Nic share when the time was right. Until then, she'd finish her birthday dinner. There had to be cake for dessert, and as long as she kept eating, kept her mouth full, there were no conversations she had to have about football players, star gazing, or falling in love with her best friend.

CHAPTER 18

SCHOOL HAD KICKED CASH'S ASS all week long. He'd barely seen Nic since dinner at her folks'. She was swamped at work, and he was on a mission to nail a statistics exam. Finally, Friday had rolled around again, and he was ready to blow off some steam. But the trouble with going to a smaller school was that there were only so many places to go, and when trying to avoid someone, it became impossible. He'd been avoiding Mira and Jaycee all week, but now Mira had him on lock.

Cash, more or less, had been glued to the back of his pickup, leaning against the tailgate and talking to Roman and a cute girl named Liz who'd been hanging on Roman's arm all night long. Liz didn't get along with Jaycee, so Cash used her like insect repellent. Not his best move, considering Roman was five minutes out from ditching this bonfire throw down, and he hadn't seen Nic yet—

Well, crap.

Mira and Jaycee had decided it was time to say hello.

Out of the corner of his eye, he saw Brandy's car rolling over the grass and parking. Talk about timing. He took a long

144

pull off his beer, avoiding eye contact with the tag team coming his way, and watched to see if Nic had ridden out with her roomies.

"Cash. Roman." Jaycee stood close enough to Roman to make her point. "Liz."

Roman shook his head. "Play nice, Jaycee."

She turned and pouted glossed lips. "What fun would that be?"

Mira laughed. Liz rolled her eyes and clung tighter to Roman.

"Where have you been, Cash?" Mira took a step closer.

"Senior year's kicking my butt." A lie, but whatever. "I've been around."

Roman looked sideways at him. "Yeah, where have you been? I thought he'd been with you, girls."

"Nope." Mira made the word pop, keeping her lips like an O a second too long. "Not with us."

In the distance, Nicola, Brandy, and Hannah walked toward the bonfire, laughing and dancing to the music thumping into the night. They saw him and Roman and waved.

The nights were cooler as September came to a close, but it was still warm enough to get away with the short-shorts that Nicola wore. He was lost from the current conversation, completely one hundred percent focused on Nicola. Mira and Jaycee both had on some absurd getup. Skirts. Fancy shoes. Way too much makeup. But even from way over here, he could tell that Nic rocked simple sexy. Sweet-ass shorts and a shirt. Plus flip-flops that neither of the girls in front of him would have ever worn. It made Nicola all the more attractive.

"Cash." Jaycee's voice called him back.

"Yeah?"

"So?"

He had zero clue what he'd missed. "What?"

"God, you're annoying. We're getting out of here. Bugs and shit are too much. Seriously, it's fall. Shouldn't they have all died by now?"

Whatever. He didn't care. "Have fun."

"You coming with?"

"Nope." He shook his head.

Two pouty faces looked at him like he was insane. They both whined and complained. But the reason was over their shoulders, dancing with her friends, hair swinging back and forth. Goddamn, Nicola was going to be the death of him.

"Whatever." Mira smirked at him.

As they retreated, Liz curled around Roman. "Good. Bye. Ugh."

"Bored with them?" Roman asked, ignoring Liz.

"Something like that."

"Well, something's going on with you. Every time I see you, you're hanging with Nic."

A boulder the size of the bonfire settled in Cash's throat. "Yup."

Roman was silent. Cash was silent. Liz wasn't. Thank God. She started in on Jaycee, and that was the perfect distraction.

Roman crossed his arms over his chest, leaving Liz abandoned and scowling. "If not Mira and Jaycee, then who?"

The fire was yards away, but Cash's hot-under-the-collar feeling increased by the second. "Why's there have to be someone?"

Roman's eyes narrowed. This wasn't going to go well. As if on some piss-poor karmic clue, Nicola turned their way. He only saw it out of the corner of his eye, but Roman looked at her for a long moment then tilted his head.

Cash drained his beer, trying for casual and feeling as obvious as a neon sign. Shit.

Clearing his throat, Roman stepped closer. "Is there—"

Another TKX who Cash would kill later, Andrew, moved close to Nicola and wrapped her in a hug. It was harmless fun. Nothing Cash cared that much about but it distracted Roman enough from finishing his question. The pause also gave Liz her in. She wrapped her arms around Roman and whispered into his ear.

"Be back in a few minutes." Roman was already walking away. Liz giggled.

Right. A quick nod goodbye, and Cash was alone. Relief was immediate except for that churning guilty feeling gnawing at him.

He pulled his attention back to the fire. Andrew had moved on after his overly friendly hello. Nicola and some girlfriends had their arms in the air, singing and dancing to music. His eyes locked on hers, and she smiled. One of the girls around her called for him to come over. He shook his head. After losing his cool at her birthday party, standing anywhere close to a dancing Nicola was trouble.

But she wasn't a mind reader. Still putting on quite the show, she was girly-drink fueled and vodka brave, calling to him as she danced. It wasn't like a strip tease. Her clothes, as little as they covered, stayed in place. But she watched him as though no one else existed, like she was dancing for him, promising his every fantasy. He pitched his beer and weighed the options.

Nicola spun around. The bonfire's light danced over her long legs, her ass. Cash sucked a deep breath. To hell with resolve. He was over there in a second. Her hands rested flat on his chest, her body moving against his. There was no control when it came to her. The inches between their lips were disappearing, and the closer she got, the more he knew he'd kiss her. His heart hammered, and his fingers flexed into her, pulling her tighter, slowly moving through the desperate seconds until his lips touched hers—

"Ow! Damn it!" Brandy shrieked.

Nic-kiss trance broke. He cursed under his breath and took a step back. Brandy was on her ass, holding on to her ankle *and* her drink. Job well done on that at least. "You okay over there?"

She scowled. "Does it look like I am, Cash?"

Ha. As much of a pain in the ass as Brandy was, at least she was entertaining.

Nicola and her friends crouched on the ground, offering a bevy of random questions and suggestions. *Walk it off. What happened? Hold it up? Put it down. Did you fall?* All of which, Brandy ignored.

The hows and whys of Brandy's tumble didn't matter. Really, Cash should thank her. His heart still raced from that almost lip lock. He focused on the positive. "At least you didn't spill."

She looked up, a genuine smile forming. "Amen to that." Then she downed the rest of her drink.

The girls pulled her up, and Brandy tried to put weight on her ankle, flinching. "Stupid country bonfire. Why the hell do we do these?"

He stepped closer. "Come on, let's see." Her ankle was swelling. "Two choices. You're sticking your foot in a cooler, or we're heading back to ice it."

"No!" she whined, wobbling on one heel that she never should've worn out there in the first place. Trying to walk, she fell over. He wasn't sure if that was more the injury or the hooch, but either way, the night was done for her.

"Your call. Rock crutches in style on Monday, or you can ice it."

Brandy's mouth dropped open. Nicola giggled. No way was Brandy going to hobble on crutches if she could help it, that much he knew.

"Well, I'm not sticking my foot in a beer cooler."

He shrugged and bent to pick her up. "Into your car we go."

After the crutches threat, Brandy was done arguing. "Hey, Andrew." Cash called over to the guy. "Can you carry Brandy?"

That was icing on the cake. Brandy smiled, playing her injured victim card as Andrew swooped in for the hand off. Within seconds, there was giggling and flirting, and Brandy tossed her keys to Cash.

"You okay to drive?" Nicola asked.

Nic, swaying, was not okay to drive. But he was. "Yup. I'll get my truck tomorrow."

149

A few yards away, Brandy was safely tucked into the passenger seat of her car and laughing loudly.

"Only Brandy can get a date out of a sprained ankle." Nicola laughed too, then whispered, "You almost kissed me."

He pulled her under his arm and started toward Brandy's car. "Could say the same for you."

"Maybe."

He looked back toward his truck. No Roman in sight. "Roman's going to figure it out."

"I know."

"Mira and Jaycee are going to figure it out," he said. They were halfway there.

"Bitches."

He chuckled. "Easy there, killer."

"Cash!" Brandy hollered from the car. "I'm ready to go!"

Nicola bumped against him. "Guess that's our cue to hurry."

In the dozen yards it took to get to the car, they'd picked up Hannah and another girl, who crammed into the backseat with Nicola.

They all sang to the radio while he drove, and his phone vibrated in his pocket. He pulled it out as the girls hit a chorus. *Roman.* When they all took a breath, he accepted the call. "Hey."

Brandy chose that moment to attempt a high note. *Wow. That was bad.* He laughed.

"What the hell is that?" He could picture Roman holding the phone away from his ear.

"That'd be Brandy."

A long silent second passed. "So, it's Brandy?"

"What?"

"Never thought she was your type."

"Jesus, dude. It's not Brandy."

Brandy leaned over. "Not me, what?"

"Nothing." Cash shook his head at her before talking to Roman again. "Anyway. What?"

"I meant to mention, I ran into our poker buddy at the Stop N Go."

"Ah." He looked at the girls in the back seat, but they weren't listening to him. "What's Gary up to?"

"He said you're doing him a favor."

Cash changed lanes, easing back toward campus. "Yup, I am."

"Does this have to do with those shady games he's caught up in?"

Basically. "He knows I can play, and he couldn't come up with the moolah. He needed something. I needed something. We made a trade."

"What'd you need?" Roman asked.

Well, fuck. Walked into that one, hadn't he? "It's nothing. I have to pony up some bank, but we both know I'm going to walk away with more money than I came with. Not a big deal."

"What's not a big deal?" Nicola asked from the backseat, clearly paying attention now. Her eyes were on him in the rearview mirror.

"Taking Brandy home." Damn it to hell. Lying to Nic wasn't on the to-do list tonight. But she, way more than Roman, wouldn't be thrilled that he was playing poker with sketchy dudes his friend was scared of.

Brandy shrieked over a new song on the radio.

Roman laughed in his ear. "Nicola will have your ass for doing her roommate."

"Probably right. If I was. Which I'm not." Dropping his head back against the rest, Cash had nothing. Well, except for a reputation.

CHAPTER 19

TONIGHT WAS POKER NIGHT. CASH had helped Nicola study and had dinner with her and her roomies, then he'd begged off. They let him go for no other reason than they had some god-awful Wednesday prime time reality television show to watch. Basically, a group of high maintenance women were auditioning for love. Seemed like a nightmare to him. Then again, there was a dude having sex with all of them on national TV, so he had to give the guy credit for that. Cash still didn't want to watch it.

The poker game was at a ritzy hotel, and he had the room number with directions to go on up. The elevator door opened, and he ambled out, catching his reflection in a mirror. The swanky hotel was nicer than any place he'd ever stayed, and he looked like a college bum with a cowboy hat. That was exactly the look he was going for.

A wad of cash weighed heavy in his pocket, and even if poker didn't make him nervous, the company he was heading toward might. When he arrived at the designated door, he knocked and centered himself, mentally wiping away anything that might let his opponents size him up.

A big guy opened the door. "What?"

"I'm here to play."

The guy looked him up and down, then stepped to the side, holding the door open. He tilted his head, and Cash's eyes followed. Typical poker table setup. Nine opponents encircled the card dealer. Each player had a mountain of chips. They looked like pros, some hiding with hats, some with sunglasses despite the smoky, dim light of the hotel room. It'd taken him over an hour to get there from campus, and though he was early, these guys looked like they'd been there for a while.

"Who's the new guy?" A guy growled at the table.

Hello to you too.

Poker was a game of skill and science, at which Cash was a master, and he was already learning who the players were. He categorized every breath, twitch, and bead of sweat. He'd never played with this *crowd* before, and besting pro players wasn't anything new for him, but this game was nothing but criminal. He had to play six hours. Then he was free to leave. Simple. The game organizer would take twenty percent, and Cash kept whatever he won.

As he took his seat, he could see why Gary wanted out of this game. In front of him was a stack of chips equal to the minimum buy-in: two thousand five hundred dollars.

"I said," the man growled again, "who's the new guy?"

Cash scooted closer to the table, pulled down his hat, and tossed in the opening bet. "I'm Cash."

A few nods and hellos.

"Where's Gary?"

"He couldn't make it."

There were a few more somber nods as though what Cash said had a much heavier context than his buddy not wanting to lose his ass in poker.

"No pay, no play," came from the corner of the room. The big guy from the door, who was easily the size of a refrigerator, stepped away from a shady figure smoking a cigar.

Cash nodded and pulled out a wad of bills. Without acknowledging him, Refrigerator man scooped up the money, carrying it back to the corner. The cigar smoker gave the dealer the go-ahead, and without missing a beat, the dealer started sliding cards. The betting began, but Cash already knew how most of the men would bet. He cupped his hands over the cards, bending up the corners enough to see the color and number.

The first hand began as Cash expected. Nervous Nelly made mistakes. A poker shark overplayed his hand and fell hard. A few others were good, but not good enough, and he saw through each of their moves.

Cash turned over a pair of Aces—the best possible hand—and his toughest opponent threw his cards, face down, into the center.

The man stood. "Tell Gianori he got my money this week, but next time, I'm not leaving empty-handed. I don't care what whiz kid—" He glared at Cash. "He brings in to screw with me."

Refrigerator man and the cigar smoker said nothing, and the bested player stormed out. No one else dared to tangle with Cash, opting to fold every time he made a raise, and his time flew by.

The man in the corner puffed his cigar. "Last hand."

Cash folded and counted his chips. After the cut to the dealer and the buy-in, his pocket would be well-lined. *Very* well-lined. He should seriously consider playing high-dollar poker more often. This could pay his rent for a couple of months.

A few minutes later, as he headed out with his score, cigar man said, "Hey, Cowboy."

Cash turned. "Yeah?"

"We'd like to see you next week."

The game reeked of bad decisions and easy money. It'd be fun, but Cash could see himself getting sucked in. A game of calculation and analysis where he made buckets of money? Yeah... But Nicola was the only addiction that needed to occupy his time. "Poker's not my thing. But thank you."

The tip of the cigar flared, and another smoky cloud billowed. "You did well."

He shook his head. "Nah, just beginner's luck."

His plan tonight had worked out well: play smart, keep his head down, read the others, and make his moves.

Cigar man stood. "Come back."

Adrenaline spiked in his veins, arriving too late to be a high from the game. If it came to fight or flight, Cash knew he could take almost everyone in the room. "This was a onetime deal for my friend."

"Wait." The cigar man motioned. Mr. Refrigerator lumbered over to block the doorway.

Jaw locked, his fists bunched. "What?"

"We have a tight-knit *business network*. You'd fit in well. We're always looking for men to bank for our team."

The way the guy said it struck him funny. It sounded like code for the *mob*, and come to think of it, these guys looked like they fit the profile. "Poker's not my thing." He just happened to be killer at it, and had no interest in running with small-town Gambinos or whoever.

"Take my card. Consider it an open invitation."

Cash unballed a fist and took the card, shoving it into his pocket along with the wad of bills. "Thanks for the offer."

He stepped around the big guy and let the door slam behind him. *What a crazy night.* He called the elevator. It was there in a flash, and he hit the button for Lobby. The descent was short. The elevator stopped a few floors down.

A hard-jawed man boarded, eyed him, then nodded toward the fat pocket. "Poker, huh?"

Trusting no one, especially after a game like that, Cash ignored him.

The man continued, "A good player has a sharp eye. Plenty of patience."

"Something like that." The guy was just as broad as he was. Cash had to give it to the dude. He looked imposing but still had a let's-chat attitude. It was odd. "Business brought you here?"

Nodding, the man said, "Recruiter meeting."

"Recruiting for what?"

"Army."

Ah, that made more sense. Cash nodded back.

"Ever thought about it?"

"Military? Nope."

"You should." The man stepped closer. "Athletic requirements wouldn't be a problem, I assume. Poker winnings pushing out your pocket says you're smart and calculating. We could use men like you."

Whoa, eagle eyes. Cash took a step back. "You don't know me."

"I know what it takes."

"We've been in the elevator for ten seconds."

He laughed. "And I've got you pegged. Don't I?"

Cash shrugged despite the bull's-eye guess. "Life's got different plans for me. But thanks for your service."

The man extended a card to him. "If something changes, let me know."

Shaking his head, Cash hadn't been more sure of the way things were going than right now. "I'm good. Thanks though." He paused, looking the guy over. "You joined the Army because someone handed you a business card?"

They reached the lobby. The recruiter shook his head. "No. I joined because life crapped on me, because I needed direction and structure, because somehow, someway, I needed to take all the anger in me and do something that wasn't self-destructive."

Well, hell. That was pretty damn honest. "And the Army did that?"

One curt, military nod. "Saved my life."

Manners more than anything else pushed Cash to accept the recruiter's card. He pocketed it next to the mobster's card and his winnings, then walked out with the guy and wished him luck. Seems like anyone who had to have the Army pick him off the ground and save his life needed a little bit of luck. Then again, what the hell did Cash know, and who was he to judge?

CHAPTER 20

NICOLA FELT HER BOSS LOOKING at her from the doorway before she knocked. She'd been snooping around the computer network and getting nowhere.

"We need to talk," Aleena said, arms crossed.

Nicola smiled, quickly exiting from programs she shouldn't have been in. "Sure. Just working on this pile." She tapped the file folder in front of her. "Trying to catch up."

"Wonderful. I appreciate that you're working hard. I just want to make sure you're not distracted."

"Distracted?"

"Yes. I'm notified whenever electronic folders and files are accessed. You have a very specific role, using only specific files."

Well, shit. Busted. She could feel the heat crawling up her neck. "I…"

"You've wandered around the computer network."

"Yes, I was just looking—"

Aleena shook her head. "Doesn't matter. Besides, I'm sure you've found that most everything is password protected."

"I was just wondering—"

"No one's asking you to interpret. No one's paying you to analyze. You are strictly moving transfers and—"

Seriously, if there was a problem, why wouldn't they want to know? "What if there's a mistake?"

"There's not."

How would she know? Everything Nic read was in Italian, and she knew her boss had a very limited understanding. "But—"

Aleena's eyes narrowed. "If you'd like the internship to continue, focus on your job, not on mine. The only thing you need to remember is *get it done.*"

Get it done? Ugh.

That was *the* most annoying phrase ever, especially when Aleena repeated it constantly, even had it memorialized in trinkets and motivational office decorations.

After Aleena left, Nic couldn't focus and decided to email her mom. She BS'ed about something Roman had said earlier and talked about Hannah's attempt at cooking them dinner. Big fail. Then she couldn't take it anymore. She had to talk to her mom about this stupid job. *If this place is cooking their books, I think I'll drop the internship and redo something next semester.*

She sighed, hit sent, and—the email didn't send. The damn Internet was out. What the hell? This job would drive her to insanity. The router was in Aleena's office, and she had to go in there to reset it. Considering nothing she needed to do needed the Internet, she was screwed. At least she had class soon enough. Maybe then she could stop obsessing over her work puzzle, which was quickly becoming very perplexing.

CHAPTER 21

CASH SPOTTED NICOLA IN THE back row of the huge lecture hall. It was unlike her to sit in the rafters, and she hadn't glanced up once to see whatever the professor droned on about. He slipped up the side stairs, scooted across one row, stepped over another row, and whispered, "Boo."

"Hey." Her eyes lit with her smile. "What are you doing here?"

"Coming to steal you for lunch. Let's go."

"I'm in class."

"And clearly gleaning all kinds of information."

Her hand slapped over the notebook. "I am."

"BS, sweet girl. I saw you, and you weren't learning a damn thing." He lifted her hand. Whatever she was making notes on, it had nothing to do with the linguistics professor up front.

"Maybe. Okay, let's go to lunch."

It was also very unlike Nicola to ditch class. "What's all that?"

Nicola shrugged. "Stuff."

Someone turned around and hissed at them to shush.

He threaded his fingers into hers. "The cafeteria's calling your name."

"Okay." She gathered her notebook and threw it in her bag.

Pulling her over a back row of chairs, he led her out the auditorium before the professor turned around from the white board to see their escape. "Alright, spit it out. What's going on?"

"I was trying to figure out these numbers from work. They don't make sense. I—" She shook her head. "I know it's not my business. But it kind of is."

"So maybe there are things you don't know about."

She rolled her eyes. "I'm doing their accounting. It's black and white. X should equal five bucks, but X is pulling more like fifty thousand bucks." Her phone rang. She looked at it and gaped. "It's work."

"Well answer it."

"If my bitch boss yells at me one more time—"

"She won't."

"You don't know the lady. Something's not right upstairs."

"Then let it go to voicemail."

She answered it. "Hello?"

Nicola's brows pinched. Nodding and um-hmming, she didn't say a lot before hanging up.

"So?" He locked his arm around her neck. "What says the evil bitch boss?"

Nicola's brow furrowed. "Um, she said thank you."

"Thanks? For?"

"She said that I uncovered a discrepancy that they'd been

missing. That there was an accidental multiplier. So five bucks was really five bucks. Not whatever I just said."

He nudged her with his shoulder. "Great. Good job, Nic."

"I don't know."

"You don't know what?"

She shrugged. They continued down the hall in silence.

"Nicola?"

"Yeah, I don't know why, but it feels shady. That was so convenient."

"Okay…"

"I mean, seriously, I start nosing around, asking questions. My boss tells me I'm wrong. *Emphatically* tells me I'm wrong. I never see anyone else who works there."

"So she didn't want to look like an ass. I get it."

"No." She shook her head. "It feels all wrong."

He threw his arm around her. That stupid we're-friends hug. The only one he could get away with, and damn if he didn't hate that right now. "Tell me what you really think."

"That my boss is stealing stuff."

"Really?" He stopped and pulled her in front of him. "Don't nose into trouble. If you really think that, then call the cops or whatever."

"Maybe."

He squeezed her shoulders. "Why the hell not?"

"Because if I'm wrong, I look like a jerk, and I've dragged a perfectly bitchy woman's name through the mud. I'd feel awful." She sighed. "You don't think her phone call was a little too convenient?"

"I think that you're thinking way too hard about a job that doesn't pay squat and is distracting you from school. And I think you're riding close to the crazy train line, Miss Paranoid."

Nicola sighed, rolling her eyes. "Maybe you're right."

Or maybe not. But he sure as hell didn't want her sticking her cute butt into someone else's problems.

CHAPTER 22

BACKPACK SLUNG OVER HIS SHOULDER and his girl under his arm, Cash led them down the hall, still uneasy about Nicola nosing around at her job. Mira and Jaycee rounded the corner.

"Tits McGee and friend alert," Nicola said under her breath.

The more he saw those two, the more annoying they got, and the more Mira went on a full court press to figure out why he'd been ditching them. Cash changed directions, playing like he hadn't noticed them barreling his way.

"Cash!" Both Mira and Jaycee said, ignoring Nic.

Damn. Escape plan not smooth enough. He turned slowly, hiding under his cowboy hat, and Mira was up in his face before he could say *whoa*.

"What's your deal?" she snapped at him.

"Ha." Nicola took a step back, amused smile playing on her face and watching his headache unfold. At least she wasn't the jealous type.

"Mira. Good seeing you." He started toward the exit again. Nicola still looked entertained and walked an arm's length away. Mira followed, sidestepping angrily, keeping pace with him.

"What's gotten into you?" she asked then looked over to Jaycee.

Cash shrugged, keeping his eye on the real reason he'd fallen off the party circuit. "Nothing."

Nicola's phone rang. She fell away, answering it out of his hearing range. Mira's smug smile made him want to shake her.

With Nic gone, Mira closed the distance. "You're never around anymore."

He moved away. "Yeah, I am. Just not..." *Screwing anything that walks. Entertained by the Mira-Jaycee triple X show.* "Around."

She came closer again, and his gentleman gene stopped him from physically moving her away.

"I thought we've been having a good time."

"We did." No reason to lie. He wasn't trying to hurt her feelings, but he wasn't going to make something out of drunken hookups.

"*Did.* And now you're done?"

"Yes." This was getting old. Straight ahead, Nicola ended her call when a football player walked up. If there was one, there were more. He'd been avoiding Jacob for no other reason than he needed to tell the dude he'd been out of line back at Nic's birthday party. Well, sort of out of line.

"Cash?" Mira gave an exasperated sigh. "Pay attention to me. We're talking."

"Mira, look." He met her gaze, trying to impart the truthfulness in what he was about to say. "I didn't know we had to talk this out. It was fun. You're fun. We all had fun. Alright?"

She pulled on his arm. "But you're done?"

"Yes. I'm sorry if you thought there was more to it." He really wasn't trying to be a dick. He glanced at Nicola. "I gotta go. Okay?"

"Oh, no. No freaking way." Her gaze locked on Nic. "You cannot possibly be serious."

Cash sliced a look back to her. "What?"

Mira scrunched her face. "Nicola Hart? Seriously?"

And he was done. "Go to hell, Mira."

Nic waved goodbye to her football buddy and smiled at him, walking back over.

"You know she's dating Jacob."

"She's not."

Mira smirked. "Kind of a goody-two-shoes."

The hell she is. "No one asked you."

"Hey." Nicola stepped close to him and threw an annoyed glance at Mira. Her look mirrored how he felt. "You ready?"

"How's Jacob?" Mira's voice was sickly-sweet.

To his surprise, Nicola smiled. Hugely. "Fabulous, I'm sure. Though you probably know better than me. And how's the rest of the football team? Baseball? Soccer too?"

"Bitch."

"Wow, Mira. You're a class act." She snickered and leaned over to him. "Roman's on his way to meet me here."

Code deciphered: don't get into a pissing contest with Mira because he wouldn't be able to walk away from publicly laying claim to Nicola. He nodded.

"We gotta roll. Nic." He took her by the elbow, they

167

turned back toward the door he'd been inching to reach, and there was Roman. Of course. Mira was still right behind them.

"Nic. Mira." Roman nodded to them, then turned to Cash. "You go to psych today?"

"Yeah." And if he could get Roman to walk away with him and Nicola, it'd be a very good thing. No need to rehash a missed psych class when Mira was ready to lob any number of accusations.

"Roman." Mira caught up to them. "I've always heard your opinions of all Nicola's boyfriends. Nothing to say on... Jacob?"

For the seconds it took Mira to pause for dramatic effect, Cash felt a surge of unease in his chest. Not for him and Roman, but because Nicola was so damn convinced things had to go according to her big reveal plan. But then Jacob's name came out, and he wanted to wrap Nic in his arms and tell everyone to fuck off.

"Nic's not a moron, and Jacob's not stupid." Roman didn't slow. Thank God. But he did look at her. "Where'd you hear that anyway?"

"Just chatting with Cash."

Roman held the door open for the girls, raising his eyebrow. "Oh yeah?"

He shook his head. "Mira's on crack."

Mira smirked. "Cash is an asshole."

Jaycee laughed then waved over her shoulder as she left. "I'm out of here guys. See you later."

"And I'm not getting in the middle of something between you two," Roman said.

Cash shook his head. "Nothing to get in the middle of."

"Right." Roman laughed. "Let's go, Nic. We'll leave these two to bicker amongst themselves."

Nic glared at Mira, sent him a questioning look, but he had nothing to offer. Mira was mad and doing a damn good job at guessing where and why he'd been preoccupied. He needed out of this situation pronto. "I forgot a book back in class."

"I'll take good care of him, Nicola." Mira's sing-song voice was going to earn a beat down courtesy of Nicola.

Shaking his head and shrugging goodbye, Cash bailed on Roman and Nicola going one way and tried to leave Mira standing there.

"You aren't even going to hold the door for me?"

He turned around and took a couple of long steps to hold the door wider. "Look, what do you want?"

"You." She batted her eyelashes in what he could've sworn was an attempt to be more like Nicola.

Didn't work. "It's not like that, and you know it."

"Since when?" Her glossed lips pouted, and this theatrical production was borderline absurd.

Just when shit couldn't suck anymore, Brandy pushed through the door looking perfectly disgusted with him. "Brandy."

"You're an ass," she said and kept moving.

Hell. Brandy's ice cold glare caught him off guard. Then again, he was in Mira's face. Any number of ways that could be taken. He took a step back. "Brandy, wait."

"Gotta go to class. Have fun with Mira."

Fuck.

He turned, about two seconds from losing his cool with the girl set to rub her tits all over him.

"Yeah, have fun with me." Mira smiled. "Come on, Cash. Stop being like this."

He looked back at Brandy, barreling down the hallway, cell phone now pinned to her ear. "Just back off."

Pushing past her, he pulled out his cell and called Nic. That beep-ring noise, the one that said she was on the other line, trilled in his ear. Damn it, Brandy was on the phone with Nicola. He was sure of it. Not that Brandy knew something was happening with Nicola, but she had to suspect something after his throw down with Jacob.

Voicemail picked up.

Hey, it's Nic. You know what to do.

Nothing he could think of sounded right, and he hung up. His hands itched to do something while his mind worked double-time. He needed to rehab his rep. How the fuck was he going to do that with—he scrolled through his phone again and hit send.

After one ring, Jacob picked up. *Kind of surprising.* "What?"

"Double-deuce, I'm an asshole."

Jacob laughed. "No shit, dick."

"We cool?"

"Never weren't."

"Alright. See you around." Cash hung up the phone and didn't feel like that conversation had done much to rehab anything that Roman would give a shit about, but at least he'd ditched Mira.

CHAPTER 23

NICOLA HAD ABANDONED ROMAN IN the cafeteria and then listened to Brandy's theories as to why Cash couldn't be trusted, none of which she believed. With each passing day, she wanted to march up to Mira and tell her to find some other hard body to cling to, that Cash was hers, in no uncertain terms. That day was coming, but it wasn't today. So she needed a distraction from slut puppies chasing after her man and decided to focus on her newfound accounting obsession.

Today was the day she would catch up at work, the day she'd show initiative and try to get Aleena to stop hating her so much. It wasn't in Nic's nature to fail, and certainly not to fall behind and not meet her goals, no matter how ridiculous her deadlines were. Her boss had extended an olive branch by admitting that things were wrong—*Just as I'd thought*—so the least Nicola could do was pick up the pace the way Aleena had all but begged her to. What better way to show a reciprocal olive branch than by working extra hours?

She pulled into the office parking lot and saw several dark

SUVs with dark windows. Maybe all the fabric-buying action happened when she was at school. This was the most cars she'd seen there. Good, she could meet some buyers or at least get a feel for someone besides bitchy-face Aleena and the rarely there receptionist.

Nic parked her car and got out. She grabbed the office door, pulled, and it didn't budge. *What the?* She knocked on the glass and cupped her eyes to peer in. The lights were on, but each knock went answered. Aleena's fancy-schmancy car was there, and Nicola pulled out her cell, still knocking.

Bam.

The noise startled her and a gaggle of birds that'd been sitting on the nearby fence. They took off, squawking. The noise, the *bam*, was like a car backfiring, except…different. She looked in the parking lot, expecting some 1970s hoopty to roll in, backfiring and sputtering. But nothing. The entire afternoon was almost eerily quiet.

A chill ran down her spine. She couldn't explain it and didn't think anything was particularly wrong or that Aleena was in trouble, but her sixth sense said, get the fuck out of there. She'd call back in a little bit. *From the road.* And if she didn't answer, maybe she'd call the cops and say she'd heard something weird, ask them to do a welfare check or whatever.

Not bothering to look over her shoulder, she kept her head down, slipped into her car, and let the conspiracy theories somersault through her brain. By the time she'd hit the main road, she was convinced she was processing payments for drug shipments or—the echo of that *bam* fired in her memory again—guns? Her stomach dropped. No way. There was nothing worth admitting or thinking about or overreacting over.

———————————

CASH WAS SEATED ON HER front porch when she arrived home. Still absolutely creeped out from her unannounced visit to work, she just wanted to get inside and let him distract her. Rushing from the car to the door, she bypassed him, only offering a come inside as she passed.

Nicola threw her bag by the couch. "Hey, Brandy."

Her roommate glared. "Nic. *Cash.*"

"Leave him alone." After the phone call about Mira from earlier, Brandy was on the warpath.

"Maybe."

Cash followed Nic down the hall to her room. Once they were both inside, she shut the door and leaned against it.

"Hey. Hi. I've…" She shook her head.

He stepped close, hard body leaning into hers. "Brandy's pissed at me."

Nicola shrugged. "Every day it's someone new. Just your turn."

"She thinks she saw something she didn't see."

"What was that?" she asked, even though she'd already heard a full report from Brandy.

"Mira hanging on me."

At least Cash was honest. "The girl's a skank."

He tilted his head. "Mira's not thrilled things have

173

changed. *But* change is what I've been after, so noticeable is good." He kissed her, soft lips making her melt against him. "So what happened at work that made you freak out?"

Yeah, her phone call to him had to have been illogical. *Meet me at home. My mind's hearing things when there's nothing to see.* The conversation had earned her nothing but a Ghostbusters joke, but he'd taken her seriously enough to get to her place before she was even home.

"Nicola?"

"I think I heard something that—" Was she losing her mind? What did she think she'd heard? A gunshot? That was ridiculous. "I'm stressed out. My job is making me a little Looney Tunes."

Brandy banged on her door, and she jumped. She wasn't sure if she was still on edge from the weird *bam* or if it was the door jumping while she leaned against it, but it made her crawl out of her skin. Again. She needed to seriously calm down.

"Nicola?" Brandy called through the door.

"What?"

Cash took that moment to kiss her neck, sliding her hair back and letting his hands drift over her shirt. "She's going to think it's odd we're in here."

"Probably not." Nicola sucked a breath when he bit her skin. "She knows."

Cash stilled. "What?"

"She figured it out. And I didn't deny it."

He stood upright. "So we're good, and we're telling Roman?"

She couldn't tell if he was happy to stop hiding or

annoyed that his big plan to brainwash Roman's lifetime of man-whore memories hadn't happened yet.

"I can hear you two talking," Brandy said through the door.

"Better than hearing something else." Cash laughed.

Nic smacked him in the chest. "You're awful."

"Ew. All right. Hannah and I want to know if we're still on for dinner at your folks' this Sunday."

Cash walked over to her bed and sat on the edge.

Nicola opened the door. "Yeah. Cash, you want to come?"

Brandy walked in, giving Cash the evil eye, but then plopped next to him on the bed.

"When has anyone not wanted to have dinner at your parents' place?" he said.

"Wait." Nicola groaned and leaned against the wall. "I can't go. I'm studying all weekend for an exam. But Roman will still head that way. Go with him."

"Maybe." Brandy shrugged. "So anyway…"

"I'll let them know." Nicola felt an inquisition coming from Brandy. She opened her door wider, giving her roomie the signal to go. But Brandy didn't go. Nope, she turned to Cash, evil eye still rocking, and made some kind of humming noise.

Cash smiled. "You okay over there?"

"I know," she said.

An instant blush took over Nicola's whole body. She felt it flash under her skin. "Alright already, Brandy."

"I know you know." Cash's smile grew. He was getting a kick out of this. Fabulous.

"Okay." Nicola opened the door as wide as it would go. "Everyone knows something. Out please."

Brandy didn't budge. "If you hurt my friend, I will hurt you, Cash."

Nic cringed. "Brandy!"

"I'm serious." She shrugged.

Cash crossed his arms over his chest. "Hey, sweet girl, give me a second with Brandy."

Brandy scowled.

Hell, this was a bad idea. "Cash…"

"Just one minute."

Now was her turn to cross her arms over her chest. "One minute. Brandy, don't be awful."

"No promises."

Nicola walked into the hallway, sighing.

"Can you shut the door?" Cash asked.

Popping her head back in, Nic felt her eyes narrow. "Neither one of you gets to be nasty to the other."

Cash shook his head. "No worries."

"Fine."

Nicola shut the door and went into the kitchen. She grabbed a glass and filled it with OJ, downing it before she'd put the juice back in the fridge. It helped her think. What were they saying? She heard the door open down the hall, and she put the empty glass in the sink. Rounding the corner, she almost bumped into a shell-shocked Brandy. The evil scowl was gone. No smirk. And was that…a smile?

"What was that all about?" Nicola asked, completely caught off guard.

Brandy looked back toward where she'd come and cocked her head. "He's a good guy."

What? "*I* know that." Nic's eyebrows pinched. "You were the one who didn't."

"And now I do."

What?

Brandy's phone rang, and Nicola headed back into her room, confused, curious, and concerned that Cash had somehow brainwashed her friend. He was sprawled on her bed, looking like it was no big deal.

"What did you say to her? She's all…nice."

"Not too much." He kicked his shoes off and tucked a pillow under his head.

"You had to have said something."

"Shut the door."

She did. "Open the door. Shut the door. Kinda getting bossy."

A lopsided grin teased her. He patted the bed. "Sit down."

Again, she did as requested. "Bossy."

"Beautiful."

Her stomach flipped. "Tell me what you told her."

Cash watched. His blue eyes shone, and he tugged her closer to him. "I told her all of the sudden every song on the radio was about you, that some things are meant to be."

"Wow." She curled into the crook of his arm. "You said all that to knock down her bitch level from raging to nonexistent?"

"I said all that because it's true. She's your friend, and I like that you've got her. I like that she wants to protect you."

"You're a really good guy."

"You already knew that."

"No, I'm serious, Cash. You're…you've always been. But this? Us? You're a good man."

"Nah. Far from it. I've done stupid stuff. I've said the wrong thing, avoided the wrong moments, and I'll probably make you want to scream and tear your hair out."

She kissed his cheek.

"What was that for?"

She kissed his lips. "You're perfect."

He chuckled. "You know what?"

"Hmm?"

"I'll never forget the exact moment I realized I loved you."

Tunnel vision. *Shocked* tunnel vision that made her dizzy. "You love me?"

"Of course, sweet girl. Are you crazy?"

Her heart beat one loud, long thump at a time. "Crazy enough to love you too."

Did she just say that out loud? Did he? She'd been in love with him forever. And ever and ever. But could she pinpoint the moment? Probably not. Just like she didn't have to remember to breathe, loving him was a part of living.

He wrapped his arms around her. "Good. Glad we cleared that up."

Tucked close to his chest, hugged deep in his embrace, everything made sense.

"You remember my senior Homecoming?" His voice rumbled, low and quiet.

Nicola smiled. "Talk about a night I couldn't ever forget." Strings of lights had sparkled overhead, glittering like stars. Cash had been announced as Homecoming king, and the queen had all but thrown herself into his arms. He'd smiled, danced one spin around, stopped, spun again. And turned.

It had all happened in slow motion. His sapphire blue eyes had found Nicola's across the room, and the slow thump-thump of her heart had catapulted, exploding in her chest. Blood rushed up her neck, her cheeks blushed hot, and her stomach had dropped all the way down to the heels she was trying not to pass out in. Because with an audible, collective gasp from their classmates, Cash had abandoned the Homecoming queen and was walking toward her, hand extended and a half-lazy, half-cocky grin that only Cash could manage hanging on his perfect face.

Every pair of eyes in the room had shot from him to her. Whispers swirled, but she hadn't cared. His eyes held her in place. His lips made her almost cave in on herself. And then his hand touched hers. A jolt of electricity had sparked at his touch and traveled up her arms, leaving a path of pinpricked skin. He clasped her hands in his, and not a word passed between them. He'd simply pulled her with him onto the center of the ballroom floor.

She sighed into his embrace. Somewhere on the sidelines, there had been a Homecoming queen plotting Nic's death. But she hadn't cared. That was one of those moments she'd remember for the rest of her life. But years later, why was Cash talking about it?

Nicola closed her eyes, remembering how real that moment had felt. How she convinced herself that it hadn't been all pretend, that the angst and desire hadn't been just one-sided and all in her mind. Cash's hands had slid down the silk of her dress, and she remembered holding her breath.

"I think you're dancing with the wrong girl, Cash."

His lazy grin hitched on the side. "Nah. She's got the crown. That's all she cares about."

Nic had taken a good look at the Homecoming queen. "She wanted a little more than that crown, I think."

"Too bad I don't care." He'd pulled back, just long enough that she noticed her heartbeat. His eyes were piercing, locked to hers, and if she hadn't known better... He'd pulled her closer, whispering, "The only one I wanted to dance with was you."

With another squeeze, she had melted against his chest and let the twinkle of the lights surround her. Yes, that night, she'd been in love with him. No questions.

Coming back to the moment with the warm, fuzzy memory, she nodded against his chest. "What about Homecoming?"

"That was the night I knew I loved you," he said softly, but she'd never heard anything more solid and strong. "You were in my arms, and the world faded away."

Her head spun... That night. Those feelings... "All I could think of was fairy tales, what I wished and wanted and was so scared to go after."

"What was that?"

"You."

He let his lips drag slowly across her cheek, not kissing.

More like grazing, like he couldn't stand not to touch her. "Me. So now you have me. Now what?"

There were a million ways she could take that. Now what? *Kiss me?* Now what? *What's in our future?* "One day, we get to happily ever after."

CHAPTER 24

GOD HELP HIM, NICOLA WAS so damn cute. She'd never been shy. If anything, she had a tough girl edge. She'd almost had to have had it, running with him and Roman her whole life. But when the sweet side came out? Those were the moments when he could see her walking toward him in their hometown church. "Happily ever after, huh?"

Her cheeks pinked, and a quiet smile grew on her face. "Maybe."

"No backtracking now. You've already said it. It's out there."

"Stop." She nudged him.

"Nah." Turning, he loomed over her, pinning her to the bed. Blonde hair spread out around her head. Brown eyes looked away but came back again. "So you're saying I'm a keeper?"

Wiggling under him, she kissed him and tried to escape. "Maybe."

"Goddamn, you're gorgeous." That stopped all her wiggling, all her playing, just locked her to him, and he stared at everything right in his world. "Tell me you love me."

"I'm in love with you, Cash Garrison. Have been my whole life."

His chest warmed as he watched her full lips promise each word. She smelled like flowers, and he nuzzled her neck, feeling her body arch underneath and loving that breathy sigh that always came when his mouth touched that spot.

Her lips parted, and when he pressed his to hers, their tongues danced. Something possessive clicked deep in his heart. His soul. Her presence was intrinsic to his existence. He loved her, couldn't stand to be without her for a minute.

It was that real. That deep.

The room felt warm, felt like desire. He was turned on and not giving a damn that Brandy could knock at any moment. "Whole life?"

She nodded, and he leaned up enough to snag her shirt off. A pretty, pink lace bra held full breasts, showing her nipples. His mouth found their tips, and Nicola made a tiny noise that he wanted to hear again and again. The lace scratched his tongue, but her softness made him hungry. Unclasping her bra, he slipped it from her, dropping it on the floor.

"Your turn." She tugged at his t-shirt. "No clothes for you."

"Getting me naked, huh?"

She nodded, smiling, biting her bottom lip. "Please."

God, she killed him. He yanked off his shirt and watched her stare at his chest, at his stomach, at the bulge in his jeans. Arousal made her eyes dark. Innocence made her eyelashes flutter.

Cash leaned over and unsnapped the buttons on her black pants. They were her standard go-to when she went to work.

He bet she thought they looked responsible, cute, professional. Whatever. She had no clue how much he loved them, how they clung to her ass and melted onto her hips. She'd throw on high heels, and he'd have a hard-on for hours. His fingers trailed the cool fabric down her hip bone, over her thigh, knee…slowing down to a crawl, he took her calf, lifted her ankle to his mouth, and kissed.

"These are some sexy shoes." He slipped the heel off her foot, laid it down, then freed her other foot. "One day, you're going to have to keep them on."

Her mouth formed an O, and he worked his way back to her zipper, sliding it down. Then he toyed with the top of her pants. Hooking his fingers on each side, he slid them over her hips, leaving her in a pink lace thong.

"My heels on?"

He could see the thought play in her head. "Maybe later."

The lace was too much—too tempting—or maybe it was what was underneath. He tossed her pants and stared at the lingerie-clad beauty in front of him. Shoes were for fantasy fucking, hot and creative, rough and wild. None of that was right now. This was about loving her, about showing her everything he felt, needed, wanted, now and later, connecting them in a way they could never forget.

He kissed her lips, her face. He buried himself in her breasts, memorizing their swell and the way she moved when he ran his tongue over the rigid tips, the way she murmured when he squeezed and nipped.

His tongue trailed down her stomach. His hand cupped her sex, rubbing the lace and enjoying how wet and aroused she was. Cash traced his tongue along the waistband and tugged the scrap of fabric off, sliding it so slowly. The inside of her thigh was soft. His palm smoothed over her skin, and he moved between her legs, ready to kiss her until she screamed.

"Cash…"

He hovered over her sex, his fingers teasing her folds. "Yeah?"

And when he parted her, her head fell to the side. "I…"

He slid a finger into her, her wetness making the intrusion slide. One finger and two. His thumb circled her clit, and his ear ached to hear each heady sigh. Slowly, he pumped into her, loving how her knees pressed against his shoulders, and when he ran his tongue along her seam, her back arched, legs squeezing.

He looked at her as she opened her eyes. "This is…" Her breaths panted. "All new to me."

He kissed her, savoring how she tasted, and ran his tongue around her clit. "That's new?"

"Yes."

He sucked her and delved with his fingers. She squirmed, and he held her in place with his arm and his mouth, working his way to her opening and kissing her.

"Oh, God." Her fingers threaded into his hair. "Please."

As he alternated, fingers and tongue, her body tensed, and he pushed her to come for him. Then she bucked and pulsed and moaned his name like this was the greatest thing he'd ever done. And maybe it was.

She dragged him up her body. The girl was on fire; he did that to her. God, he loved that. As quick as he could, pants were off, condom on, and he leaned over her.

Her hands were on his cheeks. "Let me…"

Whatever she wanted, she could have. Done. No questions asked. "Anything. Just tell me."

She took a deep breath and rolled her bottom lip into her mouth. "Be on top."

For the second that it took his mind to process, his brain to picture, all he could do was grin like a fucking idiot. Then carefully, he rolled them over, and Nicola was naked, resting on his thighs, with a nervous, so-sweet-it-might-kill-him look.

"You okay?"

She looked at his cock, then looked at him. "I…"

He put his hands on her hips and she rose above him, using a hand to position him. Then, holy hell, she lowered down. Down and tight and inching him to his death. "Fuck, Nic. Just—" He sucked a deep breath, unable to think. His eyes pinched closed in goddamn ecstasy.

"Okay?" She used his constant question and turned it on him.

Where to even begin? "Yes. Good. Great. Goddamn." He opened his eyes. She stole his heart. "Amazing."

He moved his hands. She rocked her hips, her breasts swaying. Her eyelids closed, and she found herself. Confidence and excitement building, Nicola mesmerized him. His hands ran everywhere he could touch. Her heavy breaths matched his until he couldn't take it anymore, wrapping his arms around her back, thrusting into her, and climaxing as she did, as her muscles squeezed him tight, rippling around his cock.

Their breathing seesawed back and forth. He slid one hand up and down her back and wove the other into her hair. He told her every imaginable thing he could think of. It wasn't the first time that'd happened. When they came together, it was like truth serum. But every word he could think to say came out as, "I love you."

"I love you too."

And all was right in his world. They laid there forever. She might've fallen asleep. He might not have cared. Never had he ever thought something could feel as perfect as she did.

Nicola took a deep breath, resting her chin on his chest. "We have to tell him. Tonight. No more waiting."

He nodded. No more waiting was right. "Tonight. We'll all go grab a beer. It'll be okay."

"I don't care if it's not. I'll text him." She rolled off him and reached for her clothes. She looked down at him. "But you're right. It'll be fine. Maybe."

"Roman's my best friend, but you're my life. Everything will work out. Promise." He hugged her tight. "Believe me?"

"Absolutely."

He got up, trashed the condom, and pulled on his pants. Nicola groaned with her phone pressed to her ear.

"What's up?" he asked.

"Voicemail from work." She rolled her eyes. "They didn't know that I was there earlier and left. They want me to come in early tomorrow." She ended the call and began texting. Roman probably. "I can't keep up."

"So quit. You don't need them."

"I know. It's just…"

"What?"

"I hate to fail, hate to fall behind. The whole thing's occupying my thoughts."

He tossed a pillow at her. "Well, you can't go to work

early. You have class. Besides, something freaked you out earlier."

Chewing her lip, she was thinking way too hard about that internship. "I completely overreacted. Like, big time. I'll go back today. Knock some stuff out. It'll keep me occupied before we tell Roman."

He chuckled. "Roman's not going to be that bad."

"Ha. Yes he will. He's the most overprotective brother I've ever seen."

Cash tilted his head. "True."

"I love him like crazy though. It never really bothered me until—" She pointed her finger at him and her, back and forth. "Until this."

"Really, you're over thinking this."

She buttoned her black pants. "I'll focus on work."

"Work is what's working you up. In addition to Roman."

"I've just got odd ideas in my head. It's my overactive imagination. I've been poking around, and really, I'm a self-fulfilling prophecy. I keep thinking things are true because I'm looking for corroborating evidence that'd fit."

"Corroborating evidence?" He laughed and grabbed another pillow to toss at her.

Her phone rang, and she held it up. "Roman."

His stomach jumped. "Answer it."

"Hi." She nodded. "Well, how about you meet me and Cash at High View at nine tonight?"

Still nodding, she agreed to something and hung up.

"Nine tonight?" he asked.

Her eyes were wide, and her lip rolled into her mouth. "Yup. Oh my God. I'm nervous."

"Nah."

"I am. Oh God. Okay, I'm going to work. That'll occupy me."

And I'm going out too. "Sounds good. Pick you up beforehand." He nodded. His nerves were going a million miles an hour but not for any reason she could probably guess. With a quick kiss, he jumped up before he could slow down and think tonight through. "Love you."

And he was out the door.

CHAPTER 25

PARKED AND HEART PUMPING, CASH drummed on the steering wheel with his thumbs and thought about the wad of cash in his wallet. He jumped out, slammed the truck shut, and pushed through the store's heavy door. A woman in a black suit and megawatt smile greeted him. Behind her, a very large man in a dark suit hovered.

"Hi, can I help you?" She didn't do a once-over of his jeans nor his wildly out of place cowboy hat.

"I need a ring."

She smiled bigger, if that was possible. "A ring?"

"*The* ring."

"Congratulations."

They exchanged names, went through the cursory details of how he met Nicola. Then he recounted their story and the plan to talk to Roman later that night. The woman looked like she'd turned into a puddle of goo. Honestly, he'd been expecting a bit of a lecture or for her to salivate over the easy sale. But he got neither.

She sighed. "I don't think I've ever heard a story like that before."

He shrugged. "I'm not saying I'm going to give her the ring today. Or even this month. But I like the idea of having it. When the right moment comes along, I'll be ready. Boy Scout's motto or whatever."

"When you know, you know." She sighed again. "Let's get started."

Cash looked at case after case of rings. They were pretty but not right. Worry etched in the back of his mind. What if the right one didn't jump at him?

"I have an idea," the woman said.

Minutes later, a dizzying display of loose diamonds and random bands lay on a black velvet pad.

"What do you think?" She had tweezers in her hand, and every time she moved something, she used them. The whole thing seemed odd. Actually, the last hour had just been surreal.

Working his jaw back and forth, Cash saw that the options were more than he'd expected. Now, he could see why there were all those commercials about *building* her the perfect ring. He took a deep breath. This process was complicated… But Nic wasn't complicated. She was classic and to the point except when he had her alone. Then she was near shy and insanely sweet. The perfect combination. How to translate that into a piece of jewelry?

Closing his eyes, he ignored everything that wasn't important. When he opened, he pointed. "No, no. No. No and no."

There. That was easy.

The woman smiled and tweezed away the bands and diamonds, leaving a classic solitaire and band. She picked up the band, tweezed the diamond in place, and held it out. His stomach jumped. Perfect. "Done."

"Really?"

"It's perfect."

She folded her hands together, looking pleased with his selection. "That's a memorable ring."

Memorable. Unable to wipe the grin off his face, he knew that was exactly what he wanted. Like he'd gained some kind of super powers, he felt invincible, bigger, stronger, more of a man than he had his entire life, and all because of moving forward on a very easy decision. One day, Nicola Hart would be Nicola Garrison.

He walked out the door with a ring in a bag and pulled out his phone. He hit the number on speed dial. It was picked up on the first ring.

"Hey, it's Cash."

"Hey, buddy." Nicola's dad had been just like his dad his whole life except Rick insisted on a first name, and his dad generally responded to Dad. "Nic and Roman aren't here. I heard you're not coming for dinner this weekend?"

"Nope. But I do need to come see you."

"Sure. Come on over whenever."

"Can we keep this between you, me, and Janet?"

Rick paused. "Everything okay?"

"Yeah, yeah. Just wanted to run something by you."

"Sounds good, Cash. Swing by whenever. No big deal."

"Right. See ya." No big deal. *I'm only going to ask if I can marry your daughter one day. That's all.*

NICOLA PARKED NEXT TO THE same dark vehicles and marched straight to the front door. No amount of odd noises or weird vibes would slow her down. On a mission to do right by her job, to catch up and do what was needed of her, she shelved all apprehensions and pulled on the front door. It opened, and thank God, because in her need-a-distraction-from-Roman focus, she'd forgotten that the door had been locked earlier.

Some lights were out. Some were on. No one was around. "Aleena?"

Nicola flipped a couple switches and heard nothing. Cars in the lot but no people milling around? She walked into Aleena's office. There was the next folder of papers she was supposed to work on, and more work was her distraction goal. She grabbed it, uncovering a pink notepad. *Nicola*, underlined several times, stared back. And under her name—her heart stopped. Underneath her name was a list:

Janet- mother
Rick- father
Roman- brother
Cash- family friend?
Hannah- roommate
Brandy- roommate

What. The. Fuck? What was this? A background check? It was a little late for that. And her roommates and Cash?

Nicola sunk into the chair, staring at the paper. Apprehension choked her thoughts. What did that all mean? She jumped up, looked out the door. The office was still silent. She shook. A protective anxiety pulsed in her veins, and turning back to the desk, she moved fast, checking drawer after drawer. For what, she had no idea. She tried to wake up her computer. That didn't matter. She didn't know the password. Didn't know—

She thought about Aleena's life mantra, thought about that favorite phrase as she stared at it on a motivational paperweight. Nicola's fingers trembled as she typed in GetItDone.

The screen came to life. With unorganized movements, she scrolled through the emails, did a quick search for her name. Several emails popped up, all with the same last name. Gianori.

Noise filtered down the hall from the warehouse. She quickly closed the screen and shut down the questions at the back of her mind.

Voices echoed down the hall, and maybe Aleena was in there. Maybe Nicola should march up to her and demand to know why that list had her loved ones' names on it. She walked around a row of stacked pallets and saw several men in suits. A garage door rolled open, and a small group walked in. Wait. Were those children? And they were upset? What the hell was happening?

A woman's voice pulled her attention back to the men in suits, and Nicola pressed up against the pallets, spying through a small space.

The woman shook her head. "No! Why do they have to be here? Not my babies. No!"

Oh my God. What was happening?

A large man took a menacing step toward the mother. "Shut up!"

The children were pushed toward the woman. She wrapped them in her arms. Nicola saw a man tied to a folding chair and straining to get away. He shouted at the men that he didn't know or hadn't done something. They ignored him, and the tied man used his head to direct his family away.

Nausea tore her stomach to shreds, and doom weighted her in place, unable to run away. Nicola couldn't make her body leave. Amid the screams and pleadings, Nicola wanted to make the scene stop. But her eyes were glued and her mouth sealed.

The men looked angrier. More agitated. Aleena walked into the warehouse. Nicola watched her carry ugly green folders, identical to the ones she'd been working on, and hand them to one of the men. He paged through the files then threw one at the tied man. The mother screamed and lunged. Men held her back. Shouts volleyed. Accusations and promises escalated.

Then the man who'd received the folder walked away. The mother, still held back, yelled to the kids, "Look at me. Watch me. Look at me!"

Oh no. This couldn't be happening—

Bam!

The gunshot blast echoed throughout the warehouse. The man in the chair was gruesomely dead. The woman sobbed, the children cried, and Nicola gasped, falling backward, clattering back on her butt.

"What was that?"

Fast footfalls came her way, and she ran. Out the warehouse door. Into the office.

The name Gianori popped back into her head. It all

became clear. That name fit in with the likes of Gambino and Capone. That was it. Gianori was a mob name that made the news. The Gianoris were famous. But they *weren't* in nowhere, Virginia. Except they were.

She rounded the corner toward the glass door. Two similar-looking men were strolling toward the front door, coffee cups in hand like there hadn't just been a *bam* and people screaming. She slowed to a walk, tried not to hyperventilate, but she was crying, so what did it matter? She wiped her face, looked at the ground, and tried to walk by unnoticed.

"Hey," one of them called.

"Goddamn it," came from another man flinging open the office door. "Get her."

Running as fast she could, gunfire pinged out a taillight and her trunk. She dove behind the car, crawling into the passenger door and over the center console. Not bothering to look up, she turned the ignition and blindly screeched through the lot. Gunfire blasted into the side of her car. A tire exploded. She screamed, barely able to see through her tears. Her car went uneven as she rounded the bend onto a wooded road. The building's view was obscured from the main road—

She screamed again. A black SUV with flashing lights swerved in front of her. She hit the brakes. Other SUVs sped by. Two men dressed out of an action movie—black tactical gear with big, huge guns—ran at her. Nicola screamed and cried and threw her hands in the air because who the hell knew what was happening?

They opened her door, grabbed her like a rag doll, and

half-carried, half-ran her to the SUV's backseat with a hand slapped over her mouth. She couldn't breathe. Couldn't scream. Finally, the gloved hand moved off her mouth, and she gasped for breath.

The action figure peeled back his hat. "Nicola Hart?"

Still gasping for breath, she nodded.

"I'm FBI Special Agent Hamilton. You have one minute. Listen carefully."

She choked on a breath. "Okay."

"You've been working for the Gianori family."

She nodded. "I just found out." She had to tell them about her family. About the list. About the murder she just saw. Her stomach lurched. She pointed, still unable to catch her breath. "They—"

"We thought we'd get there in time."

She shook her head. Somehow, that made it even worse. She could barely breathe for all the sobs.

The man's face pinched, and he looked toward another agent in the driver's seat. After their silent conversation, he turned back to her. "You are the only person who knows details on their network. We need your help."

"Help?" She wiped her face.

"Nicola. Listen to me." The agent's firm stare bore down. "We need your help to make sure that never happens again. We need to learn what—"

"But I don't know anything."

"You know more than you realize."

"They just murdered a guy in front of his children." She sobbed again. Then panicked. "They have my family's names."

"I know."

What? She struck the man's chest. "You know? You know!"

"The Gianori crime family is…" He braced her, sitting her back in her seat. "I'm sorry you were sucked into this."

Maybe she was in shock, because that violent execution repeated in her head over and over. "They killed—"

"They will kill you too."

"What?" she shrieked.

"And your family. Loved ones. It's what they do."

Nicola pushed away from him and slapped on the door for the handle. "No."

"Do you know what witness protection is?"

"What?" She pushed back again. "No! I'm not doing witness protection. You have to—" She choked. "Leave everyone."

"They've got your family pegged. Your boyfriend."

"My boyfriend?" No one even knew…

"There's a hit order on all of them if you—"

"What?" She couldn't process any of this.

"You have one minute to decide. Help us out, you will be safe. Your loved ones will be safe. The Gianoris will think you're dead."

"Dead?"

He nodded. "Easiest thing would be car accident— explosion—given how you tore out of that parking lot."

"And if I don't?"

"Then they get away with murder. Again. The murders that you helped cover up. You'll forever wonder when they're coming for you. Your family. And they will."

"No." She cried. "Why didn't you find me sooner? Why didn't you stop this?"

"No one expected this today. But it happened. Take a deep breath, and think. You walk away, but your family lives. You will protect them. You'll save them." He paused. "No one wanted this to happen the way it did. But it's done. We have a plan. We can make this work, but decide now."

"Now?" She sucked in a deep breath, mopping at her eyes, her nose. "I need to call—"

He shook his head. "You can't."

"But—"

"Not if this is what you decide. Save your family. Help prosecute those fucks."

Her mind froze. The pink post-it note with the names listed floated in her memory. As if she needed additional prodding, the agent handed her pictures and papers. Cold, hard proof that the Gianoris were evil, evil people. Dead bodies. Crying families. Newspaper articles.

"Don't let this happen to your family."

The next photograph was of her parents. Her jaw shook. Tears ran freely. "I can't. I'm not strong enough."

"Last chance."

"This isn't fair," she moaned, but the man said nothing.

Finally, he nodded. "It's not. But the Gianoris have to think you died. Your family too. Save their lives."

Falling into a blubbering heap, she nodded.

"It's the right thing to do. The only thing." He turned from her, speaking toward the front seat. "Let's go."

Their SUV began to drive away, and she pulled away

from him, staring out the window. Her car, without her in it, rushed around them.

"Wait. My purse. My phone."

The man shook his head, and whatever else he had to say turned to white noise. She was dead inside.

CHAPTER 26

LAID OUT ON THE COUCH and housing a sleeve of crackers, Cash concentrated on ignoring that stupid-awesome smile that kept creeping up on his face. Twice, Roman asked him why he grinned like a fairy. Twice, Cash had realized he smiled like a lunatic. The guy hadn't connected Cash's over-the-top mood to drinks with Nicola tonight. T-minus two hours, and everything would be in the open.

A knock at the door startled him. Roman was closer, so he stood and answered it. "Hey, Ray."

Raymond was a TKX who'd graduated last year. He had lived in their frat house when they'd been freshmen and had made sure he and Roman didn't go through too much hell while pledging. Not that the dude had been nice about it, but he had been decent.

Cash stood, walking toward the door. "Ray. What's up?"

Raymond was in his cop uniform, his face paler than Cash remembered. "Can I come in?"

Roman stepped back, and Cash's stomach dropped.

Ray looked sick, ill, ready to fucking die on the floor, and something very bad was about to happen. Dread spiked in

Cash's blood. Certain disaster loomed, and he didn't know why.

"I don't normally do this. But." Ray swallowed, and Cash watched a knot travel down his throat. "It was her. And you two—"

Roman stepped forward. "What?"

Terror tingled in Cash's fingers, made his lungs ache and his arms go numb. "Ray?"

"Nicola was in a bad car accident. It careened off the road, caught fire."

"Fire?" Roman coughed out the word.

Cash couldn't swallow. Couldn't think or breathe or function.

"There was an explosion. I'm sorry." Ray's brow furrowed.

Roman shook his head. "What do you mean *you're sorry?*"

Ray's lips were flat; his jaw ticked. "Someone's talking to your parents now."

"What hospital is she at?" Roman's voice cracked.

"She's not." Ray cleared his throat. "Nicola died."

Cash couldn't listen anymore. He walked away, his stomach turning. He was going to get sick. Nausea whipped through him, and his eyes burned. His vision blurred, and he didn't get far. Turning around, he couldn't believe it was true. But Roman and Ray were still there. He staggered to the couch, dropping. Crumbling. Falling apart. *I'm sorry... Nicola died.* It repeated over and over and over. Slapping his hands over his ears didn't help. Threading them into his hair and pulling didn't either.

Roman, shouting, brought him back to the living room. Tears fell down Roman's angry face—Cash's too—desperate and disbelieving. He'd just seen her. Just left her. Just loved her. Fuck it all, just bought her a goddamn engagement ring because he was going to marry her.

His head pounded and soul shredded. Bleeding. Dying. Pain too intense, too all consuming. Cash left them, heading to his bedroom. He slammed the door and collapsed onto the bed, clinging to the rabid belief this was an awful nightmare, that this couldn't possibly be happening.

Through the wall, Roman's angry, unbelieving shouts morphed into a heart-wrenching wail. The noise—pain made audible—was all he needed to know. This was real. This was hell, and his life was over.

Cash grabbed his phone. Hit her name on speed dial. *Hey this is Nic. You know what to do.*

No. He didn't. He'd never been more lost, ever. Over and over, he redialed, listening to her voice until exhaustion made it impossible to push the button again, and he gave himself over to black out.

———————————

THE GRAY SKY MATCHED HIS gray heart, and Cash had never been more sure he couldn't make it through the day. Roman was at home with his folks. Cash could've gone home, could have gone to their home. But instead, he stayed at his place, hoping to God this was a mistake, a nightmare, and Nic would walk through the door. He waited, watching it for days. Anyone who came by, he ignored. Just him, with a bottle of Jack Daniels, sitting on the couch, waiting until he could wait no more.

Bleary eyed, he knew today was the day he had to get up, find a dark suit, and make the drive home. Today was the worst day of his life because it ended hope. Cash swallowed, choking on the thought of burying her.

He made it to the shower, hung-over and wishing he could make the pain stop. He had to pull it together. Now. Nicola deserved better than him showing up unable to walk, swaying and smelling like booze. He scrubbed his hands over days' worth of a beard, then looked in the mirror. Bloodshot eyes and a tortured face stared back. *Just survive today. For her.*

He showered, managed to choke down some toast, and dressed in a suit he'd never be able to look at again. Stuck in a fog, he drove on autopilot to his folks' house. His dad gave him a hug. His mom cried. Everyone said how sorry they were. And they had no idea.

No clue how much he loved her.

No idea how much he hurt.

He didn't want to drive with them to the services but didn't want to sit and wait. He walked over to Roman and Nic's house. *Roman's* house. Because Nicola was gone. He didn't knock. Didn't even say hello when he walked in and planted himself on the couch. Slowly, he shook his head, remembering the last time he'd talked to Janet. Nicola's ring was in his pocket. He hadn't been far from it since he bought it the day she died, and he wasn't quite sure what he would do with it. Maybe leave it with her as she was buried? Was that a possibility? He didn't know what else to do with it. It was just an object, but damn, it meant the world to him. That ring was the only thing he had left.

Janet walked into the living room and sat on the couch. She wore a black dress, and it somehow made their tragedy all the more real.

Patting his leg, she smiled sadly, and he couldn't get any words out. Something would be appropriate. *I'm sorry for your loss. I'm so sorry.* So many people had said sorry to him, and it didn't help. So why even volunteer that trite of a conversation piece?

Janet did what moms do and wrapped him in a hug. "She loved you so much."

The knot in his throat had to have started bleeding because raw pain exploded. He should be comforting her. He needed to be the strong one. But the only thing he could focus on was the empty hole in his heart.

He opened his mouth to say something, but nothing came. So he nodded in her hug, hugging her back, then sat up and pinched the bridge of his nose.

She patted his leg. "Would you like to ride with us, or are you driving with your parents?"

"No thanks." He swallowed after finding his voice. "I'll drive myself."

Janet's brow furrowed, uncertainty painting her features. "You're family, Cash. You know that?"

He nodded and stood. "I'll see you there."

Before he collapsed in on himself, he walked to his truck. Hands on the steering wheel, staring straight ahead, it felt as if hours had passed, but he checked the dashboard, and only ten minutes had crept by.

He drove to the church and pressed against a wall in the back. Folks from their hometown, friends he hadn't seen in years, came up to him, offering condolences. They must've all thought it was like he'd lost his sister.

Tight chested, he faked a half-hearted smile when his parents walked in.

"Mom..." Words ached when he spoke, so he decided to stop doing it. Besides, the only thing he wanted to do was shout that he loved Nicola, that she was stolen from him, and that his life was over. Instead, he tilted his head toward his dad to say hello.

Like the man understood, Dad gave him a look that said enough. *Hello. I'm sorry. This sucks. I hurt too.* Because as much as the Harts loved him, his parents adored Nicola and thought of Roman like their boy. His mom's eyes were red. Her black dress, just like Janet's, made his heart hurt. Cash took his mom by the elbow, and they filed to the second row. Like the moms had an unspoken code, his mom pushed him to Nic's mom, and somehow he found himself seated in the front row, next to Roman, and staring at a closed casket. And he couldn't breathe.

The accident had done bad things to her. She'd lost control around a curve, careened off a steep edge, but they'd been assured she didn't suffer. Because if she'd been alive when her car exploded, if she'd been scared or trapped or... Pain sliced his throat, seared his eyes.

The service started. People spoke. The church sang. The room moved around him, the service unfolding, but he couldn't think. Couldn't see. Couldn't focus on anything except the casket. Besides, no one would say anything he didn't already know.

Roman stood. Cash's stomach sank, as though it hadn't done that a million times over the last few days, then he stood beside his best friend. They stepped forward, meeting four others. With Nicola's engagement ring still in his pocket, he took his place across from Roman as a pallbearer and walked down the aisle.

It struck him then that just recently, he had thought about walking down the aisle of their hometown church, but with her on his arm. As his wife. Cash took a deep breath, put in place a stiff upper lip, and did the job that was expected of him and died a little with each step.

CHAPTER 27

THERE WERE A LOT OF things Nicola had been told she couldn't do. Couldn't call, couldn't write. Couldn't drive by, couldn't have any accidental run-ins. But all of the lectures and information had failed to keep her from begging and pleading to see her family, to see Cash, one last time from afar.

The US Marshal now in charge of her life had pitied her. That had to have been what it was. But no matter, Nicola got her way. And from a faraway hill almost a mile away, tucked in a nondescript car with binoculars, Nicola watched as her casket was buried. Watched as her friends said goodbye, as her family did the same. And she watched, tears streaming as Cash stood there long, long after everyone had left.

Witness protection had been the wrong decision. But it was done. She couldn't get out of it if she wanted to, and in reality, she was saving all of them, saving their lives, saving them from physical pain and heartbreak. The more she learned about the Gianori mob, the more she knew about their history of dismembering and destroying families in a physically, painfully, tortured-until-all-were-dead way. And she'd stopped that from happening to her loved ones. She had saved them.

But Cash.

Standing there.

All alone and not leaving.

All the color bled from her heart as he dropped to his knees and stayed there. Her heart and soul fell with him. There was nothing left of her, just a shell of a person.

Her eyes blurred through the tears, and she blinked them away, failing to stop their flow.

"This isn't good for you, Nicola."

Nic looked at the worried Marshal next to her. *No kidding.* Watching wasn't supposed to help. This was supposed to hurt. It was punishment for doing what she did, no matter how much she believed it was to save them.

"Just another minute." Nic brought the binoculars back up, and she watched pain personified.

Her stomach fell again. She could handle anger. But somehow, watching the strongest, surest man she'd ever met, come apart…that was too much.

Gasping for breath, Nicola opened the car door, unable to think clearly. Her lungs ached, feeling like they pumped too fast, but no oxygen made it in. She coughed and sputtered, running from the car, unsure where she was going or what she was doing on a faraway hill.

Strong arms wrapped around her. She shook her head, screaming for this to stop. It was more than she could handle. The Marshal held her, hugged her, told her it'd be all right, eventually. Nic lost her footing and didn't try to get it back. But the man took her dead weight, let her sob, and carried her to the backseat of their vehicle.

This was all too much.

A steady voice promised her, "One day, everything will be okay."

The door shut, countering the Marshal's promise with *nothing will ever be okay.* They hit the highway, driving toward a new life and leaving the one she'd wanted since the first day she could remember smiling at Cash.

THE SILENCE WOULD'VE BEEN TOO much if it weren't for the screaming in his head. The noise was so loud Cash couldn't think about the world around him. He'd been on his couch for hours. Maybe days. Didn't matter. The second he'd arrived home from the funeral, he took off the suit and threw it away. That didn't help, so he took the trash out. Still didn't help. The ring was still with him. He'd transferred it from his suit pocket to the pocket of the closest pair of pants he could find, jeans he'd left on the floor.

His front door cracked open, allowing a slice of sunlight to come in the dark cave he'd made. Brandy and Hannah. Flinching from the light, he waved at them to leave. "Go away."

That was all the energy he had. But they ignored him. If Roman were here, they could focus on him. But he wasn't, and they would've known that. Roman's car wasn't out front.

Hannah lifted a bag from Cracker Barrel. "We thought you might be hungry."

"Nope."

"Cash…" Brandy's eyes cut him to the core.

"Just go."

Brandy shook her head. "Hannah, can you give me and Cash a minute?"

Christ. He scrubbed his face, unsure and uncaring of whatever Brandy had planned. Maybe a good dose of get-the-fuck-up. Perhaps she'd take some tips from a psych class and try to talk him into moving off the couch. Whatever her plan, it would be a waste of their time.

She sat next to him. "I'm really sorry, Cash."

"Everyone is really sorry."

"But I don't think everyone knows how in love you two were."

His eyes stung. "Fine. Big secret's still a secret."

"I think everyone thought that you guys were... Well, maybe everyone but Roman. But—"

"Brandy, I really don't need this now. I appreciate the food and all—"

"That day you told me how much you cared for her. That day—"

"*Last week,*" he growled. "That day *last week* when I thought I had life completely under control. *That day?*" When he knew what the hell was happening, where life was going. Goddamn, his throat hurt.

"Yes." It was so unlike Brandy to whisper. "The day you told me you couldn't imagine your life without her."

"Yet here we are."

"Here we are."

He reached into his pocket, wanting to show her the ring, wanting to throw it across the room, but deciding it was almost sacred. Withdrawing his hand, his fingers grazed over the edge of a piece of paper. He pulled that out instead. Not a piece of paper, but two business cards. Two possible distractions: the seedy world of mob poker and the regimented life of the military. Two ways he could go and maybe survive this.

"Cash?" Brandy brought him back to his crappy reality. "I just want to make sure you don't, I don't know, do something stupid."

Hannah walked in with a couple of plates of food. "Hey, Cash, honey. You should eat."

There were a lot of things he should do. Eating was on the list but not high enough, and that was part of the problem. Avoiding something stupid wasn't anywhere close on his list. "Excuse me. I have to make a phone call."

Both cards in hand, he headed to his bedroom, still unsure which number he would dial. Cash scraped the corner of the cards across his palm, weighing his options. Whichever one he chose would serve the same purpose: distract him until he could function or at least until it killed him.

His phone rang. *Roman.* Cash dropped his head, hurting so bad he didn't know how to live. But he answered because Roman was his boy, and he was in the same head space as him. Cash crumbled one business card up as he answered, tossing it to the trash. Decision made, it was going to save his life. Roman's too. "Hey, man. Get home. I know what to do."

THE END FOR NOW...
Until Cash and Nicola find each other again in
GARRISON'S CREED.

A look at

GARRISON'S

CREED

CHAPTER 1

SIGHTING THE TARGET IN HIS crosshairs, Cash Garrison accounted for all of the variables. Wind speed and direction. Distance and range. Now the world would be free of one more bloodthirsty warlord in less time than it would take for the walking dead man to finish his highfalutin champagne toast.

Hours had passed since Cash nestled into place, high-powered rifle held like a baby to his chest. A thousand yards out from the extravagant mansion, he'd burrowed into position, melting into the landscape, and waited for this moment. Antilla Smooth, dressed like the million dollars he made as an arms dealer and unaware of the grim reaper sighting his forehead, made his way past the French doors.

Cash caressed the trigger, knowing exactly how many pounds of pressure it would take to fire the round. He monitored his breaths and heart rate. When his entire body was still, in between beats and respirations, he'd take the bastard out. One less piece of shit strutting on God's green Earth. The world would be a better place, and Cash's job for the day would be done. He and the team could find a local bar, find some ladies, celebrate and make a night of it. *Good plan.*

He adjusted for a breeze, blinked his eyes, counted down his breaths, and—stopped. Stunned. Frozen in place. Heart pounding like a coal-eating locomotive.

A woman in a golden dress and sparkled-out jewelry that'd make royalty jealous wrapped her arm around Antilla. A soldier would sell his last bullet for a kiss from her lips. Cash saw her through his scope as though she stood a mere twenty feet in front of him.

She looked like...but it couldn't be.

His spotter spoke the direction in his earpiece. "Send it."

Cash spoke into his mic. "Stand by."

His spotter whispered again. "Eyes on your target. All conditions accounted for. Go. Send it."

Nothing. Cash didn't speak.

Earpiece again. "Go, goddamn it."

The woman slunk around his bull's-eye, her beautiful hair piled on top of her head, save for the loose pieces framing her face. Her smile slipped into a laugh. *I've inhaled gun oil fumes. I'm losing my mind right this second.*

"Cash, man. You there?" His spotter grabbed his attention, wrenching him back to reality.

"Here. Yeah, man. Here."

"Wind from three o'clock. Dropped to five mph. Hold. Target blocked." The woman draped over the man. This was a nightmare—his nightmare—blasting from the past and slapping him clear off of his prone position and onto his stupefied ass. The spotter spoke again. "Clear. Dial wind right, two mils. Send it...now."

Heartbeat. Breath. Heartbeat.

Fire.

And breathe.

Now, they had to move. Fast. He knew the spotter team should be slipping through the thick Maine forest. Cash paused and glanced longer than he needed to confirm the kill. Tuxedoed man on the ground. Kill shot. Dead. Panic attacked the room. People ran, most likely screaming. Security scrambled. Dogs loosed. Barks growing closer. But the woman. The golden silk-draped woman stood still, staring at the busted windowpane in the French doors. No expression. No emotion. Not a drop of anything.

Cash shook his head, clearing the ghost of her image, and focused on his job. One shot, one kill. Just the way he liked it. He cleared the shell and casing from his bolt-action rifle, policed his brass, and snapped to a crouch, erasing any evidence that he had spent hours in the spot. A half second later, he beat feet, sliding down the side of the wooded hill, leaving no trail.

His spotter buzzed in his ear, confirming their meet-up point. "Rendezvous at location A, twenty-two ten." He could do it. He should do it. He powered down a hill, sliding as dirt gave under his feet. Brush slapped him in the face. Vicious barking closed in. The main house illuminated day-glow bright.

Man, he was going to hear about it for this one. He told his spotter, "Location C, twenty-three hundred hours."

"Cash—"

It took a lot for Roman to break protocol and use his name over the radio frequency, but Cash knew his spotter, his closest friend, was pissed. And an upset Roman was as much fun to deal with as the dogs Cash was about to run back toward.

Not much to do except kill an hour. Cash pulled his earpiece out as Roman cursed again. Nothing good would come at the end of that sentence. Cash laughed. Radio silence wasn't the best road to take, but it was better than coughing up an explanation of the impossible.

NICOLA GLIDED AROUND ANTILLA SMOOTH. His lifeless face stared at the ceiling, and his perfect hair hid the sniper round's entry wound. Given the crimson puddle painting the white carpet round the backside of his brain, the bullet was a through and through, and her night was ruined. Her operation ruined, completely FUBAR.

Chaos filled the room, and she was the calm eye of the storm. Everyone and everything swirled around her. Loud noises. Screaming people. Security moved fast, but what was the point? They'd failed.

She hadn't failed, but the last few months were now crap, and it was time to call the powers that be. They'd be interested in this turn of events. Nicola put down her champagne flute and pulled out her cell. She walked away, feeling her smooth silk gown train trailing behind her.

The phone rang once, and a surprised voice answered. "It's a little early for our chat."

"We should get together for ice cream." Nicola gave the

phrase that told Beth, her handler, that this mission was dunzo.

Beth didn't miss a beat. "I have to run errands first. I'll meet you after you head to the dry cleaners."

Dry cleaners. Yup, time to turn into a shadow and slink away. It was the right move, pulling her home. Too bad she had nothing to show for the months spent playing to the dead megalomaniac's ego. She'd been so close, only one or two days away from locking down the international players in Antilla's arms network.

"You've got it. I'll be in and out first thing in the morning." She walked down the hallway, and a guard looked. Apparently, her saunter was too calm, given the way other women shrieked their horror. "*Ciao*," she said goodbye, keeping up her Italian persona and putting a hand against her throat.

She looked at her designer gown. No blood. At least there was an upside to this evening's party. That and she wouldn't have to feign interest in Antilla, the sick prick, then backpedal when he wanted to take her to bed.

Personal preference. Some ladies in the Agency did what they had to do without a second thought. She'd had second thoughts. And thirds and fourths. She'd wanted to screw Antilla Smooth like she wanted a root canal done by Kermit the freakin' Frog: choppy marionette hands flopping up and down.

"Gabriella?" Someone used her alias. "Gabriella, are you okay?"

Nicola saw a butler who had been friendly to her since they'd arrived at Antilla's Maine estate. Her name poured off his lips, imitating the Italian flare she used when introducing herself.

"Yes, fine. *Bene, grazie.*" He looked unassuming. Who

knew why the man worked for Smooth Enterprises, but looks were deceiving. Trust no one. "I need to step outside. Fresh air."

Really, she needed to get out of Maine, but why elaborate? She slipped outside. The night was daybreak bright with the estate's security system fully engaged. Her hand caught her eye. The fluorescents made her olive skin look green, not complementing the dress she'd fallen in love with. Nicola weighed her lack of options, knowing she'd need transportation and, for the moment, not knowing how she'd secure it.

A chill spiked over her skin as a gust blew through the forest. Someone was still out there. The same someone who took out her mark.

Pop. Flash. Pop. The exterior lights died, and she was left to her thoughts in the moonless night. Another chill rolled over her shoulders. No wind this time. She pivoted, reluctantly ready and willing to ruin her dress and take it out of the ass of whoever was to blame. Her muscles tensed. Her eyes adjusted in a flash. A man. Large. Broad. Armed. Twenty feet away at the side of the patio.

He spoke, the baritone timbre coating her in a hurt she'd hidden years ago. "Nicola."

She didn't need to see his face. His voice shattered any semblance of strength she'd mustered. Nicola braced one leg back, prepared to attack. Ready to defend herself. But who was she kidding? If he laid one finger on her, it might be her undoing. All her suffering, pointless.

"Nicola," he said again. Still as firm, but this time knowing. "What the fuck?"

This was bad news of the worst variety. She pivoted back toward the doors, ready to go back inside and hash out an emergency extraction strategy with Beth. No time to wait for tomorrow's withdrawal plan.

Reaching for the doorknob, she willed herself not to run.

"It's you, isn't it?" he said.

Sweet Lord, why was Cash here? Why was the one memory she could never forget standing in the middle of her job? And why was he talking to her, armed and looking far more dangerous than the last time she saw him?

"Stop your sweet ass one second, and turn around, Nicola."

She spun on her stiletto heel, knowing she'd never be able to get to the subcompact gun tucked on the inside of her thigh. Even if she could, she'd never hurt Cash.

"No, sir. You're mistaken." She put on her best Italian accent, knowing it wouldn't fix this problem.

"Bull—"

The butler opened the door. "Gabriella, please come in. Everyone's gathering in the main hall. It's dangerous to be out here."

Cash stood in the shadows. She knew the butler couldn't see him. Yet, her pulse stuttered, and her throat tightened. She wanted to protect one man from the other. Nicola looked over her shoulder, and Cash was gone.

GARRISON'S CREED is available for purchase
at major book retailers.

ABOUT THE AUTHOR

CRISTIN HARBER is a *New York Times* and *USA Today* bestselling author. She writes sexy, steamy romantic suspense and military romance. Fans voted her onto Amazon's Top Picks for Debut Romance Authors in 2013, and her debut Titan series was both a #1 romantic suspense and #1 military romance bestseller.

Learn more about Cristin at http://cristinharber.com

CPSIA information can be obtained
at www.ICGtesting.com
Printed in the USA
LVHW051046080419
613329LV00021B/714/P